I0781115

WED TO THE ALIEN PRINCE

ACCIDENTAL ALIEN BRIDES

JANUARY BELL

Wed To The Alien Prince by January Bell

Published by January Bell

www.januarybellromance.com

Copyright © 2022 January Bell

Cover by Natasha Snow

Edited by Belle Manuel

Interior Art by lucielart on instagram

All rights reserved. No portion of this book may be reproduced in any form without permission from the publisher, except as permitted by U.S. copyright law. For permissions contact: admin@januarybellromance.com

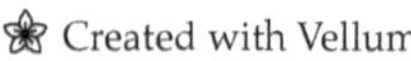 Created with Vellum

AUTHOR'S NOTE

Some themes and content may be disturbing for some readers. For a full list of content warnings, please visit my website: www.januarybellromance.com.

CHAPTER
ONE

GEN

I'M GONNA FUCKING kill him.

The thought runs through my head like it has for the last week and a half on this soupy, swamp-ass planet from Hell. The alien—who's somehow both currently number one on my hit list *and* the only reason I'm still alive—smirks at me, one fang showing in his stupid lopsided grin.

He jabbers something at me, pointing to the snare I've managed to set and spring all in one go, despite watching him carefully every time he's set one without trapping himself.

I can't understand a word he's saying, but I'm pretty damn sure 'I told you so' is written all over his stupidly handsome alien face.

"I didn't do it on purpose," I tell him, crossing my arms. My blonde hair hangs around my face, and I blow at where it tickles my nostrils, trying not to sneeze. "Stop laughing."

He's doing that odd, barking sound, smiling hugely at me now, like this is the funniest thing he's ever seen.

"I don't see you trying to catch dinner, fuckface," I tell him. It's not true, not at all, seeing as how he's made sure we're both fed, but I'm tired of feeling helpless. I also called him *limp dick* a few days ago, but since that seems to likewise be wildly inaccurate, I had to stop.

I shouldn't have even noticed anything about his dick, but here we are in alien jungle purgatory.

He prods the ground with a makeshift spear, using it to hold himself up as he laughs and responds, the argument and humor clear in his tone, though my translator completely fails to do its damn job.

"Can you cut me down?" I say, acid in my voice.

He says something else that the translator fails to provide any context for, instead spitting out gobbledygook like 'cupcake head, pretty frosting, understand bacon.'

It gives me a headache. I swing upside down, dangling by one ankle, for a moment longer. I'm loath for him to ruin the vine-y rope we spent three days braiding together to make this snare from. Well, the would-be snare, anyway.

I mean, it worked…I just didn't intend to be the thing it caught.

But this asshole doesn't show any inclination to let me down, so I swing harder, before crunching up to untie the knot—

I give a yelp as the alien's talon slices through the vine braid, the awful nightmare sensation of falling triggering near panic. I do *not* want to break a bone out here. With the high humidity and torrential rains, and god only knows what kind of alien bacteria, any kind of injury could turn deadly.

But strong arms catch me, and I suck in a breath as I look up into his green face.

"Thanks," I say, relieved not to have met the ground head first.

I wriggle, trying to get free, but he holds me fast.

He points at the vine rope, then down at the ground, shaking his head.

"Yeah, no kidding," I tell him. "I don't want to fall, either."

The alien nods his agreement, saying something else my translator tells me is 'bride fly, not cupcake.' I growl in frustration, and his arms tighten around me.

A primal roar sounds—closer than it has been the last few nights. My skin prickles, my entire body going into overdrive, screaming that something big and bad is headed our way. The alien crouches, and I try to get free of him, disliking how his over-the-top alien muscles bunch on top of me. They're huge. It's absurd. I feel tiny next to him, and fragile, and dainty, and I hate it.

I worked hard to be a badass, and he's selfishly ruining my self-image.

He tells me something in a low tone, and I grunt in irritation.

"Bad chicken hungry," the translator unhelpfully provides. "Eat cupcake."

If I could stick my hand in my ear and dig the fucking thing out, I would.

Bad chicken hungry, indeed.

He motions to the direction the sound came in, muttering something, then points in an opposite direction. We're in agreement about that, at least.

"Yeah, we definitely need to get away from whatever's screaming out there. The bad chicken does sound hungry."

A stream of noises comes from his mouth, his fangs dangerously close to my face as he talks animatedly, still pointing.

He stops, inspecting my expression, though what he expects to get from me is a mystery.

"Sure," I say, shrugging and only managing to press myself further into his embrace. "If you want to go that way, whatever. It doesn't matter, anyway."

It doesn't. I've all but given up any hope of being reunited with my friends. The first few days, I was sure we'd meet up with them, that I'd see them again soon, that they were all fine.

But I didn't.

I don't know what happened at the welcoming ceremony. I don't know why I'm alone with a Suevan in the damn jungle, and even thinking about it makes me slightly nauseated. My teeth grind in frustration.

I've been stuck in this primeval alien jungle long enough now that even the Suevan's green face is looking good. Some nights, I wish I *could* understand him, just so I wasn't so damn lonely.

But the translator they gave us is crap, and half the things it spits out are complete nonsense that only manages to give me a splitting headache.

The Suevan takes off at a fast jog, his gait so effortless and smooth that I hardly bounce in his arms. I gave up trying to get him to let me walk a couple days ago.

For some reason, the big scaly dude wants to heft me around like a sack of potatoes, and at this point, I barely have enough pride left to care. I'm hungry, I'm tired, and I'm filthy.

First Officer Potato Sack, that's me.

So I sigh and close my eyes, nestling deeper into the heat of the Suevan's bare chest.

Might as well take a nap.

KANUZ

MY HUMAN'S ASLEEP AGAIN, her breathing shallow and swift, her skin dull and pale. At first, she was all angry words and fighting, and I loved it. Her fierceness, her warrior nature—so at odds with her delicate appearance—set my heart aflame. I truly chose the best out of the human females.

But now, after the attack on our mating ceremony, my tough little human wife does not seem like herself. Even the flash of fury at being caught in her own snare disappeared too fast, and though I grew hard when she told me she would fuck my face, her verve was worrisomely short-lived.

She sleeps too much, eats too little. And still, my female does not understand anything I say.

The hunting pair of Crigomar—huge carnivorous reptiles— trumpet at each other. We should have been in Edrobaz days ago, but a flood and resultant mudslide cut us off from the mountain city.

And now the Crigomar, too far north and out of their normal range, separate us from safety and my yellow-haired mate's friends.

She misses them. She's grown used to me, yes, I can see it in the way she chatters at me sometimes, not knowing I respond in kind, waiting for her to understand me. She wants her own people. She's said as much, her full pink lips pressed thin in worry.

My little golden-haired mate acts so tough, but she has a big, soft heart. Even if her tongue *is* razor sharp.

I need to try harder. I need to start over with her. I need her to trust me.

To want me.

To be *mine*.

My teeth gnash, my fang drawing a bead of blood on my lower lip. The Crigomar roar again, the change in their tone telling me they've scented prey.

I hope it is not us.

Regardless, we need to find shelter. My mate is not as tough as she pretends to be, not at all, and her fragile human constitution is clearly failing her in the wet muck of the deep Suevan jungle. She needs rest, food, and a reason to live.

I will give her all three.

I hold her closer to me. Leaves and brambles lash at my hide as I jog through the thick undergrowth. A thin, drizzly rain begins again, and she stirs as droplets dampen her soft skin.

If I remember correctly, there is an abandoned temple near here. I did not spend as much time in the jungle as the Suevan warlords, so turning this direction for shelter I *think* I remember is a gamble. As their prince, I was instructed in many things, including survival, but was never thrown into the wilds as they were. The other warlords no doubt know this terrain like the backs of their scales, but my memory is fuzzy.

Irritation sends my tail lashing behind me.

If I had studied Suevan geography harder, perhaps my mate would already be safely ensconced at Edrobaz. Instead, my beautiful yellow-haired female turns pale and wan, her spirit dampened by the endless heat and rain.

Something snags on my scales, a thorned vine prying several from the flesh of my leg. My speed falters, and a zitsu leaf slaps against my face. I growl in impatience, casting a glance overhead, to where the asteroid belt that rings Sueva is barely visible through the thick canopy.

I count the largest of the ice and stone chunks, using the old ways to navigate.

The temple ruins may not be the safest place in the jungle, but it beats sleeping in the open. Even a crumbling roof overhead will be better than resting out here, where the Crigomar hunt and where the endless rain erodes my female's spirits and saps the heat from her body.

My hands grip my beautiful mate's flesh, and she stirs in her sleep, muttering something about cupcakes, which are apparently all she's dreamed about lately.

"That is right, little mate. Have your cupcake dreams. When you wake, I will have you safe and sound."

And I will truly begin wooing her, doing more than simply surviving and waiting for her translator to work.

Everything about our situation is less than ideal, but my attempts at soothing her are making things worse, I fear.

I will make it better.

I will be better.

Too many days I've spent wrapped up in the minutiae of my royal house, of titles and a heritage that does *nothing* for Sueva. Too long have I spent standing on ceremony instead of making a real difference, instead of bringing all Suevans to heel under the royal house, no matter what tradition dictates. Too many nights have I spent trying to soothe the ache in me with drink and females. And now, the separatist threat has driven me and my chosen mate deep into the jungle.

The tell-tale snap of green wood bent past its breaking point echoes around the jungle. A flock of jewel-like birds bursts into the air, squawking complaints into the uncaring Suevan sky.

The reptilian roar of a Crigomar booms, so loud and close that my heart hammers against my chest.

I break into a sprint.

"What the hell?" Gen asks, her eyes wide open and fiery. "That sounds like a T-Rex, which is impossible."

She stares up at me, and the beast screams again.

A muscle in my jaw twitches, my talons gripping the slick ground as I push my body further, faster.

"Bad chicken hungry," she says, her fury-filled eyes melting into pure horror. "Oh god. Chickens. The translator—" She touches her ear, staring up at me. "Dinosaurs. *Dinosaurs*? Just when I thought this couldn't get any worse."

My own implant sends an image of a scaled reptile, huge, in response to the word dinosaur.

"Crigomar," I tell her. "Di-no-sawer." I nod vigorously, trying to wrap my mouth around her strange word for the beast. Despite the fact the Crigomar are hunting us, pleasure blooms inside me.

She understood me! For the *first* time.

"Dinosaurs are out there, and you're smiling at me?" She squirms so hard against my chest that I nearly drop her, her flesh slick with the slide of rain and sweat.

"I'm taking us somewhere safe." *I hope*. She can't understand me, but I'm not about to give her any reason to stare out at the jungle with more fear.

"We need to get somewhere safe. Where something that big can't get in." Her blunt white teeth worry her lip, and I nod vigorously.

"Is that what you're doing? Taking us somewhere safe?" she asks, squinting up at me.

The fearful look's been replaced by focus, and her bravery sends a shiver of delight through me. Not many Suevans would respond as well to the knowledge the Crigomar had their scent, but this little human is thinking her way through the problem.

I like that very much.

The trees suddenly give way to brackish water, green scum

thick on top. Insects the size of my hands flit about the water on shining wings, unafraid of the creatures dogging our steps. As if I've summoned them with my thoughts, one of the Crigomar looses another explosive roar, this time closer than before.

I step into the water.

"What the fuck?" Gen's little nails bite into my scales, and I clamp down on a moan of pleasure at the strength in her grip. Now is not the time to lose myself to the pleasure of her intensity. Not at all.

"We can't go in there," she hisses. "Who knows what kind of disgusting alien bacteria is in that water. Look at the size of those bugs." Her throat bobs as she swallows.

"Sssssafe," I tell her, mangling the human word, but she still glances up at me in clear surprise. I jerk my head to the barely visible temple in the distance.

It stirs a need in me, the sight of it. Calls to some latent primal urge in me to seek the goddess, to ask for her help. The Crigomar are her creations, just as all of Sueva is. Perhaps the goddess is in agreement with the separatists, however. In agreement with my father, too.

Maybe I *am* unfit to rule.

Maybe aligning with the humans to save our species is the unholy act they claim it to be. My father gave his blessing, albeit warily, as it is the only way for Suevan life to continue.

I shake my head, setting my jaw and splashing through the green muck. Something thick coils around one of my ankles, and Gen's grip on my shoulder's becomes painful.

"That's the biggest fucking snake I've ever seen." Her eyes are round as saucers. "What is wrong with flora and fauna on this planet? For crying out loud. I need a weapon. I can't stand this."

"Am I not weapon enough?" I huff at her, annoyed at her outburst. "I am the prince of Sueva, the heir to the throne, and I am trained to defend our planet from all threats. I can easily dispatch this snake." I kick at it with a taloned foot, and it raises a thick head from the water, before disappearing deeper into the muck.

"See?" I tell her, shrugging one shoulder. "They're not as brave as you are, my ferocious female."

"Tigress?" Her nose crinkles in confusion, her translator obviously ruining my words. Again. "Are there tigers here, too?"

Weary of my inability to communicate, I sigh, the foul-smelling water now up to my knees. Ahead, the temple entrance yawns dark, mostly obscured by the thick vines. We're still a good way away, and the muck at the bottom of the stagnant water sticks to my feet. Every step is a struggle, and still, the Crigomar draw closer, judging from the way the birds of the jungle take flight, the way the treetops rustle.

I grit my teeth, glancing over my shoulder at where the creatures last bugled.

They've gone quiet, and I do not think this is a welcome development.

Fuck.

Gen follows my focus, craning her neck back to peer over my shoulder. "What are you looking for? You don't think those things are following us, do you?"

"They're following us," I tell her. "The water may slow us down, but it should slow them down as well. The temple should keep us safe. They're too big to follow us in there." I point to the stone statues that flank the opening, the carved eyes weathered by time and the elements. A root snakes from one of the statue's mouths.

She stares up at me, then squints at the temple in the distance. I see the moment my explanation registers, even though she still doesn't understand the meaning of my words.

"There's something over there, and you think it's safer?" She tilts her head, her eyebrows raised. Gen speaks very slowly, as though I'm the one having trouble communicating.

I snort my amusement. "Yes, wife, that is exactly what I think."

Her eyes crinkle at the corners, and for a fleeting moment, I think she will grace me with her smile. But her gaze slips behind my shoulder, her body tensing in my arms.

"Oh, holy *shit.*"

Something large splashes into the water behind me, and I don't have to look to know exactly what it is.

"I need a fucking gun, why don't I have my gun?" Gen asks, her eyes blazing with a vividness I haven't seen. "Nature finds a way," she says, and then sucks in a startled laugh. "Well, I never thought I'd die being eaten by an alien T-Rex, but here we are!"

I throw her over my shoulder, and she makes a soft whoomph as the breath whooshes out of her, and I break into a run, the muck and water slowing my steps.

Behind us, the Crigomar screams its frustration.

We need to make it to the temple, and fast.

CHAPTER
THREE

GEN

THE ALIEN HAULS me over his shoulder, and I can't even find
it in me to fault him for it. Do I like being slung from his shoulder
like a sentient bag of rice? No. Do I think I can move as quickly as
a being made to race through the swamp? Also no.

I'm not an idiot. My best odds right now are to stick like glue
to the scaled warlord with his muscly arm clamped around my
thighs, his tail swishing through the poison green water as he
races to the structure at the edge of the swamp.

The alien growls something at me, same as he has for the last
week and a half.

It doesn't irritate me, not now, seeing as how he's clearly as
focused as I am on getting our asses to that stone house and away
from the fucking walking museum exhibit paused momentarily
on the edge of the swamp as he sprints away. Mud and viscous
green sludge spatter my face and hair, and I brace my hands on
the alien's lower back, watching the dinosaur's progress.

"This is insane," I tell him conversationally, my heart
pounding so loud it nearly drowns out the frustrated whuffs the
T-Rex makes as its huge nostrils flare. "Dinosaurs went extinct on

Earth millions of years ago. I can't believe I'm seeing one in real life."

"Crigomar," the alien says, a hint of annoyance in his voice.

"Sure," I say. "Of course." Who am I to argue with the slab of scaled meat carrying me through a swamp like a green knight? I'll play princess if it saves me from getting eaten by the monster staring us down.

The dinosaur isn't green. In fact, it looks nothing like the T-Rex toys I played with once upon a time as a kid. Its hide is deep, blood red, with long zagging stripes of dark brown like a zebra's. I'm half-fascinated, half-terrified, and I can't help wondering why it's that color.

A movement out of the corner of my eyes catches my attention, and I slowly swivel my head, nauseated from the alien's shoulder digging into my stomach and the stink of the swamp.

At first, I think it's another one of the massive dragonflies.

And then I realize why the T-Rex's coat is red and brown. I never would have thought red would blend into the shadows, but holy shit, does it ever.

A second dinosaur jumps into the swamp, sending a fetid wave of stagnant water toward us. It opens its mouth, lined with yellowed, razor-sharp teeth, and *screams*.

I clamp my hands over my ears, closing my eyes instinctively.

"Fuck, fuck, fuck."

The alien pats my bottom reassuringly, never slowing down.

"Go faster," I tell him. "Run faster, my dude. I do *not* want to be the main course today."

He responds in his language, and the translator gives me the usual garbled feedback.

For some reason, probably because we're being hunted by *dinosaurs*, I start laughing. And once I start, I can't seem to stop. I'm on an alien planet, being carried like a damsel in distress, and for once, I actually *am* a damsel in distress.

There's no denying that this alien is protecting me, and for all intents and purposes, I'm more of a damsel than I've ever been in my goddamn life.

I hiccup a choking sob, both dinosaurs cocking their heads and watching us struggle through the swamp.

When they decide to attack, they do it together.

"Fuck," I yell. "They're coming."

The alien growls something incoherent, something my translator interprets as *making love.* I laugh again, and it's a completely unhinged sound. My hair is coated in slime and foul water, my long ponytail slapping against my cheek with every step the alien takes.

"We're not going to make it," I tell him. "We're not going to fucking make it."

His talons dig into my hip, and I clamp my mouth shut as he rattles off something in a seriously irritated voice. The dinosaurs are gaining on us, their black eyes glittering through the steady pelt of rain that seems to be the de facto weather on this planet.

The closest T-Rex suddenly pauses, cocking its head so severely that my own neck aches to see it.

"Oh my God," I breathe.

The snake my alien shook off is nothing compared to the massive thing now entangled around the T-Rex's powerful legs.

"What the hell? Has that thing been there the whole time? Does everything on this planet take steroids? Why is it so big?!" I'm squealing with the shock of the thing, the primordial part of my brain screaming to run.

Which is ridiculous, because I'm already moving much faster on the alien's back than I could run on my own. I grip his hips harder, and he makes a low noise in his throat.

The huge snake rears its head, and I'm caught between horror and fascination as it plunges thick fangs into the neck of the T-Rex. The other dinosaur roars, heading away from us to attack the gargantuan snake.

"I'm going to have nightmares the rest of my life," I say. "Oh well. It'll be a nice change up from all the Roth invasion ones, I guess. Just throw a fucking snake and dinosaur in, mix it up a little!" My laugh trickles out again, my mind wheeling.

The alien strokes a hand down my thigh, making a soothing noise.

Talons screech against stone, gunk sliding from my arm and plopping against the moss-covered steps.

"We made it."

The alien grunts, setting me down on my feet and tugging me inside the dark maw of the cave. My eyes widen as I register the stone statues flanking the entrance.

This isn't a cave, or a house.

This is some kind of alien ruin.

A chill goes down my spine. I hesitate, staring at the sightless eyes, the roots scrambling the features of one humanoid statue.

My alien tugs at my hand, and when the dinosaur screams again, I swallow hard and follow him inside. I blink, trying to get my eyes to adjust to the dim light.

"Wow," I say, staring around.

A tree, roots bulbous and huge, grows from the wall of the ruin, the hole where it's burst through the stone roof allowing a modicum of light in.

Outside, one of the dinosaurs roars again, the sound sending my heart rattling against my ribs.

The alien puts his arm around me, a stern expression on his face as he checks me over. His forehead furrows, his diamond-shaped pupils expanding as his gaze rakes across my skin.

No one's looked at me like that in a very, very long time.

Like they care.

He reaches out a taloned hand, and for a split-second, I think he's going to touch my cheek. Stepping closer, his hand closes around my ponytail, and my heart speeds up for an entirely different reason than the dinosaurs rampaging outside.

Sharp claws dig through my ponytail, and the alien grins at me, showing long fang-like canines, as he draws them away.

An enormous leech is in his fingers.

"That was in my hair?" I ask, and another rasping laugh trickles out. "Awesome. This place gets better and better."

He grins at me, too, then hurls the leech out the entrance.

"Thanks," I tell him, and I mean it. "You saved my life. And for getting the leech off me, too. That would have been… unpleasant." It's not the first time I've thanked him, despite the fact he's annoyed me more often than not, and now I have to sit with the fact I'm uncomfortable with how grumpy I've been.

It's like the near-death experience has kicked my ungrateful ass, trying to show me how much worse it could get. Like it's this planet's way of reminding me that I need to stop bitching and make the best of this.

His smile deepens, and I study him. He's beautiful, if not strange, but beautiful all the same. The massive tail and green scales are a little freaky, sure, and his bone structure is too severe to be human, but it's symmetrical and strong and a little bit breath-taking.

And that's not even touching on the muscled work of art the rest of him is.

I've been awful to this alien.

I know I have been. I need to make it right. As much as he laughs at me, the dude's kept my silly, stubborn human ass alive for a week and a half.

I slump against a hunk of jagged rock that, judging from the overhead hole, must have fallen from the ceiling.

"You can understand me, right?"

He nods slowly, his tail twitching behind him.

I clear my throat, my mouth twisting to the side as I force the words out. They've never come easy before, but it turns out that nearly getting eaten by a dinosaur has an effect on a person.

"I owe you an apology, dude." My nose wrinkles. "I've been mean to you. And you didn't deserve that."

He steps closer, and my eyes widen a little at the size of him. It's one thing to be suspended and carried around by the guy, and it's quite another to have all that shirtless muscle staring me in the face.

"And I also owe you a thank you," I say. "Several hundred of them, probably."

He shakes his head, squatting next to where I sit on the slab, so that we're eye-to-eye.

"You didn't have to save me, or take care of me, or lug me around, but you did, and as annoying as it is to need to be saved, I'm really glad you did."

His stare is intent and focused, and when he blinks, it's slow enough I can make out his third eyelid. It should be weird, but I've spent too much time with him now to be anything but used to it.

The alien shakes his head, so close I can feel his warm breath on my face. His long blue-black hair's pulled up tight in a bun, and a strand falls over one cheek, giving him a rakish air. I don't know if I'm imagining it or not, but his gaze is heated as it travels over my face.

Tentatively, he reaches out one clawed finger, tracing it down my cheekbone.

My breath catches. Is he going to kiss me? Do aliens kiss?

It hits me like a brick, then.

I don't even know his name. I am *such* a terrible person.

"I'm Gen," I tell him, pointing to my chest. "Genevieve. But everyone calls me Gen." I point to him. "What's your name?"

He grins at me, and something tells me he already knew that. Did I tell him at the welcoming ceremony? My mouth twists to the side as I try to remember. The whole thing is a blur—getting off the ship, him bizarrely feeding me, the translator being dumped in, the ship exploding…

I shake my head, trying to clear it, trying to remember, but the memories are fuzzy in the same way all my memories of the Roth invasion are—like I'm underwater and can't make them out, can't quite see or hear. Sometimes, though, I'll hear loud noises and a crystal sharp memory will surface, leaving me shaken and raw, the vision of the Roth in my mind's eye terrifying and larger than life.

And then, of course, there's the nightmares, which I can't ever seem to remember other than a deep-seated feeling of dread, of panic and the knowledge I'm going to die, dragging me from sleep as I choke on nothing at all.

The alien grips my chin, his fingers gentle as his eyes lock on mine.

"Gen," he says slowly, like he's savoring the word. He breaks into a grin.

I must be dehydrated, because I nearly swoon.

"Kanuz," he says, removing his hand to point at himself. Satisfaction plays across his face.

"Ka-nuz?" I repeat slowly, the middle consonant somehow harsher, more guttural, than what I can say.

He laughs. "Kanuz."

"Right," I say, slightly breathless from his proximity. Or dehydration. Yeah. That's it. "Ka*nuz*."

His fingers grip my cheeks, and he repeats his name again, eyebrows raised.

"Kanuz," I manage, his fingers squeezing in on my mouth as I hit the second syllable. When I say it this time, he growls his approval, his strange eyes flashing as his tail swishes behind him.

Butterflies explode in my stomach, and I'm lightheaded.

"Kanuz," I say, and he lowers his hand. "I hate asking you for help. Well, I actually hate asking *anyone* for help, which is a big personality flaw, to be honest." *Get control of yourself, Gen.* I snort, making myself continue. "I need something to eat and drink. I'm weak."

He makes a soothing noise, patting my cheek again, and the sexual tension disappears in the span of a heartbeat, gone so fast I'm nearly sure I've imagined it.

Did I want there to be tension between us?

Am I considering kissing him?

Nah. Definitely not.

Probably not.

He tugs at my hand, and I obediently follow, which is unlike me enough that I know I need some water and food ASAP. The ground is slippery underfoot, and even with my Federation issue boots, I have a hard time navigating the moss-covered stones.

"What is this place?" I ask, craning my neck to look around. Kanuz draws me tight against him, his arm around my shoulders as we go deeper into the ruin. Despite the twisted roots plunging deep into the foundation, the places where the roof's been fractured, stones tossed to the floor, there's an austere quality about.

Something awe-inspiring, something *different*. There are no windows, but huge metal sconces are set into the stone, and carvings adorn nearly every wall, so worn and weathered they're impossible to make out. A huge dais rests at the far end of the place, and our footsteps echo against the slick stone.

There's a solemn quietude about the place.

It reminds me of… a church.

"Is this a temple?" I ask, and Kanuz's hand squeezes my shoulder.

"Yesssss," he hisses, and I jerk my head towards him, shocked.

"Is my translator working? Did I just understand you?" God, I want someone to talk to, not just talk *at*. I am sick of our little guessing game. I want to *talk* to this massive alien warlord.

I want Kanuz to be my friend. I could really fucking use one. A friend.

My cheeks heat, and desire ripples through me as I give a sidelong glance to his packed-on muscles and compelling face. Okay, maybe I want more than friendship.

Fucking doesn't seem to be a bad way to pass the time until we're rescued or the roaring dinosaurs give up.

I scrub a hand down my face.

I must be losing what's left of my mind.

I can't seriously be thinking about banging the big dude.

My gaze slides to the bulge in the front of his pants, and I suck in a breath. Okay, so maybe I am seriously thinking about it. Sure, he saved me. Sure, he's been a pretty great companion on this hellacious planet. Sure, he's got rock-hard abs and from the looks of it, he's packing heat in his downtown area. Sure, his face is like, really nice to look at, for a green lizard alien.

That doesn't make it a good idea.

I'm on a diplomatic mission, for crying out loud. I can't go around fucking the aliens because they're hot and nice and I'm bored. What would the Federation say? Surely I'd be breaking about fifty military laws.

Not like that's stopped me in the past.

I kick at a rock in my path. It clatters across the floor until it makes an odd plinking sound, then a splash.

Kanuz turns his head to look at me, talking away in his growly language. The heat from his body warms mine, and now that I've had a moment to recover from the adrenaline rush of nearly being a dino-snack, I'm all too aware of it.

The dull light glimmers off the surface of the floor next to the raised platform. Vines snake in and out of the walls, and I peer at them nervously, hoping like hell that they're just that: vines, and not anymore fucking giant snakes. My stomach squirms at the thought of that massive thing, and my feet falter.

Kanuz peers down at me.

"There aren't any more snakes in here, right?"

He purses his lips, shrugging one shoulder.

"That doesn't make me feel better," I tell him. "I'm not in the mood to deal with any more prehistoric snakes. I mean, I will if I have to, but I'd really rather not."

He laughs at that, his grin lighting up his whole face, and I can't help but grin back. For a scaly green dude, he's got a nice smile. That or I'm losing my mind. Either or.

Maybe both!

I sigh, and he keeps smiling at me, then mutters something my translator interprets as BE NOT AFRAID! Which, while dramatically biblical, seems to be an improvement over what it's spat out at me so far.

When he flexes his arm though, his muscles bulging, I snort, sure he's joking, until he narrows his eyes at me, something like hesitation on his alien face.

"No, no, I didn't mean to hurt your feelings," I say quickly. Great, I'm being an asshole again. "Your muscles are very big."

He flexes again, muttering something that my translator interprets as 'not soft' I have to bite my cheeks to keep the inane laugh inside. Instead, I reach a hand out, squeezing all that thickly muscled bicep.

My eyebrows shoot up in appreciation. I'm no slacker when it comes to gym time, but this guy puts me and any other gym bro to shame. He's jacked.

"Wow," I say, finally awkwardly withdrawing my hand. "That is really something." I pat his arm, chancing a glance up at him.

He murmurs something to me, his eyes locked on mine.

I hear it then: the unmistakable trickle of water. When I turn toward the sound, I realize the glimmering wasn't the floor after all, but a long, narrow pool spanning the length of the back of the room. Water streams from an opening, and I step closer to get a better look.

"Fuck," I say, cringing back. It's not just an opening, but a huge snake's mouth, the stone jaw unhinged wide to allow the water to pour out. "That's really off-putting, to be perfectly honest." Especially after seeing how big the snakes get on Sueva.

Less than ideal for someone who isn't a big fan of all things scaled.

Kanuz's hand closes around mine though, and I realize I'm going to have to make a slight correction to that assumption.

I might be a fan of one scaled thing, after all.

CHAPTER
FOUR

GEN MAKES ME LAUGH. It is so good to see some lightness back in her step, her eyes glimmering as she discovers the oddities of the swamp temple.

It makes me feel marginally better for nearly getting us both eaten by the Crigomar.

The giant snake attack bought us barely enough time to get inside the temple, and I send up a quick prayer of thanks to the goddess for the timing of the massive beast's arrival. I never thought I believed the stories about this place, about a temple guardian, but a gargantuan snake might make a full believer of me yet.

Perhaps we have curried the goddess' favor.

Or perhaps my superstitions run deeper under my scales than I would like.

Still, I have found the fresh water of the temple, and the fountain and drainage system, no matter how antiquated, appear to be working. The Crigomar have been deterred from pursuit. We have a crumbling roof over our heads, and for that, I am thankful.

And for Gen's smiles, I am more than thankful—I am fully blessed.

"Is it safe to drink?" she asks, squatting near the rippling surface.

"Yes," I say in Suevan, then sigh once more. "Here." I crouch next to her, cupping my hand and bringing some of the crystal-clear water to my mouth and drinking. "These old temples had advanced filtration systems for the worshippers that lived here, monks, priestesses and the like—understand?"

She watches me carefully as I drink, and I keep talking to her in a soothing voice, knowing she doesn't understand a thing, but trying to calm her all the same.

"If the fountain were not running—" I point to the unhinged jaws of the snake, the defender of this place. "—then it would not be safe, because that would mean the filtration system had failed. But our ancients built this place to withstand time." I drink deeply from the pool, relishing the fresh water, the cool zip of it across my tongue. A ragged laugh trickles out of me as I run my hand across the smooth bark of one of the huge zitsu trees that's taken up residence in the main temple.

"I suppose even the ancients didn't plan for the tenacity of the zitsu." I motion to the tree, then settle my back against it and watch my pretty female. Tentative, she dips her hand in the water, scooping it out and drinking from it as I did.

"Oh god," she moans. "This tastes so good."

My cock grows hard at the noise of her simple pleasure, and I grunt. What I wouldn't give to be the one causing her to make that small sound.

Her throat moves as she swallows. Her gaze drifts from the pool to the water rushing from the snake statue.

"It's some kind of filtration system, isn't it?" Her eyes narrow, and she stands, brushing her palms off on her filthy pants. "I don't want to muck up our drinking water, but I need to wash this stuff off. I could really use a bath." The words trickle out of her, murmured so quietly I know she's mostly talking to herself and not to me.

I don't mind. I'm relieved she's talking at all. I'm relieved she isn't terrified and shaking on the floor after the Crigomar attack.

I'm pleased she has relaxed enough around me that she even considers it.

I stretch my arms behind my head and give her a toothy smile, the kind I saved for females at Suevan settlements, though none of those other species were half as enticing as this human creature before me. Her smooth, unblemished skin, the color of a ripe quarn fruit, the pink tinge across her cheeks and nose that makes me want to nibble on it, to see if she tastes as sweet.

I know she does.

I drink her in, as though she is what will quench my unslaked thirst: the full berry-red lips, her ample muscled curves, the lush fall of her yellow-gold hair. I wrinkle my nose. It's not quite as lush or yellow now, what with the muck of the swamp sticking to it.

Immediately, shame fills me.

My little human is filthy. I have not taken very good care of her.

"You should bathe in it." I don't have anything for her to get clean with. I glance around, as though some sort of cleansing oils will appear, but this isn't my palace at Perzovir. There are no servants here to wait on us, to treat my little wife as the princess she is.

"What do you think?" she asks me, pretending to rub her arms. The algae from the water around the temple crusts across her skin, flaking off as she grazes her fingertips over it.

Not for the first time, I want to find the tech that assured us the translators would be safe and effective and shake him.

"Yes," I say, nodding my head.

She repeats the Suevan word, mangling the guttural syllable, nodding her head, her eyes narrowed.

A smile breaks across my face, and I stare at her, astonished and inordinately pleased.

She says it again, and a happy laugh comes out of her. "God, I am beyond excited to get clean. This stuff—" She pulls a sheet of green muck off the back of her hand. "—smells rancid."

Sighing contentedly, she yanks her shirt off, then her pants, and I go stone still.

Gen's been shy about her body, more shy than other species I've been with before, but now? Now her body is bare save a scrap of fabric around her chest and another between her legs. She splashes into the pool, a blissful smile on her face.

"It's so deep," she muses. "Much deeper than I thought it would be."

I cannot bring myself to look away from her. I want her to say that about me. I want to be deep inside her.

She doesn't mean *that*, though. She does not know what she does to me, doesn't know that I have spent the last week and a half lusting over her, loving the chase, loving her feistiness. It is not often that a female resists my advances. It will only make it that much sweeter when she finally sees how happy I can make her.

I must be patient… but I am a prince. Patience was never a part of my lessons. My hands fist at my sides.

"I wish you could talk to me," Gen says, scrubbing at the dirt on her arms. "I want to know what this place is. Did you know I went to school for history?" She stares, waiting for a response, a response that she will not understand.

I grunt. "I would like to hear more," I tell her.

"Right," she says, and her smile turns sad, and a little lonely.

"I can hear you. I understand you." I point to my ears, then lower myself into the water. Her gaze focuses on me, and I wade out to where she floats in the middle of the pool. "I know you cannot understand me, my wife, but I want to hear more of this history you studied. History is important to my people, sacred and interwoven with our beliefs."

I pause. Water clings to her cheeks and eyelashes, and the urge to kiss it away grips me. There's something about this female, something beyond how I've felt about any of the other females I've lain with over the years. There is a softness to her under her feistiness, and it calls to me.

"It was before the Roth invasion," she says quietly. "After that, everything changed. I entered the Federation military. I had to get really hard, really fast. We all did. I think... I pushed myself harder than I had to. Everyone looked at me and thought I was just some delicate, pretty girl, and I hated it. I hated that it made me feel weak." Gen studies one of the stone snake coils jutting from the temple wall. "Once the Roth came, it was like I didn't want to be *me* anymore. I didn't want to be cute Genevieve. It felt like I couldn't be her anymore. And now I'm here. And I feel like I'm not sure who I'm supposed to be now."

She falls silent, her lips pressed thin.

I hate that she can't understand me. I hate that she's feeling this way, but I like that she's talking. I love how she is talking to *me*. Sharing parts of herself she keeps in shadow under that brittle exterior.

Of course, she likely only feels comfortable talking to me so honestly because she needs someone to listen—and knows she will not understand anything I tell her in response.

I swallow.

"I understand," I say, gazing deep into her unusual blue eyes. "For so long, I have been raised to rule Sueva. Raised to lead my people, my people who are slowly dying out, thanks to the virus. The pressure—" I pause, scrubbing at where some of the scum sticks to my scales. "The pressure to be the prince my people needed was too much. I have made bad choices. I acted spoiled. I slept my way through the other species on my trips to the settlements. I tried to prove myself against the Roth, and maybe I did, but... but now? Now, the separatists threaten everything." I take a deep breath, blowing it out slowly as I voice what troubles me most. "And I fear it is because of me. Because I have been a weak leader. Because I cannot fill my father's shoes."

I lapse into momentary silence, my father's words echoing through my head. *You do not take Sueva seriously. You do not take yourself seriously. You will not be king until you can prove you have outgrown your childish needs and selfish behaviors.* I have not spoken to my father in months, preferring instead to divert myself with the novel thought of taking a human wife, of preparing a home for her in Perzovir, our capital, and the idea of helping our species survive.

And here she is, before me, a vision in the water of the many-faced-goddess' temple, her head cocked to the side, listening, though she cannot understand the words.

She's more than I ever bargained for, and suddenly, I know I am not enough.

How could I be, when we're stuck in the jungle because of my ineptitude? By my lack of knowledge of Suevan geography, by the fact I was spoiled and cosseted and allowed leniency where our Warlords were not?

My chest heaves, and I stare at the patch of sky visible overhead, the Crigomars still roaring occasionally in the distance.

"I do not want you to look at me like that. Like he does. Like I am a weak leader. A failure. For the first time, I want to truly prove to myself who I am." *For you,* I think, but the word sticks in my craw despite our translation issues. I cannot allow the separatists to continue their nonsensical missions against us. Not when the price of their success could be Gen.

My tail lashes angrily under the water, sending a wave slapping against the temple stones. As good as it feels to unload my burden, the deepest secret of my heart, to this woman, it's painful, as though the words have been torn from me.

And she doesn't even understand them. I am not sure if I am grateful for that fact... or frustrated. I do not want my Gen to know what a failure I am. How Sueva is split because of my inability to unite our dying people.

I would hate to see the derision return to face.

I have only just won her smiles.

GEN

IT FEELS so fucking good to get clean. The green mucous-like crap that I picked up in the swamp sloughs off in disgusting sheets. It reminds me a little of a cheap face mask I bought once, except it smells anything but spa-like.

It feels equally as good to trauma dump on poor, hot, unsuspecting Kanuz. I know he can understand me, so I *should* feel vulnerable about throwing some of my deepest feelings at him, but I don't.

He didn't run away at my stream of consciousness either, like any of the dudes I dated on Earth might have.

No, instead, he said something back, in that strangely soothing alien language of his. Kanuz's diamond-shaped pupils expanded like he listened intently while I talked, and then he said something back, his face wrinkling in what looked like frustration. Now he stands in the water next to me, his giant frame easily touching the bottom, while I float and scrub at the nastiness stuck all over me.

This ruin has a weird vibe. It's not something I would ever say to any of the crew, because God knows they'd laugh at me saying something had a *vibe*, but it's true. The green swamp, the giant snake, the running water paired with the overgrown and crumbling interior... It's bizarre as hell and completely alien.

Unsettling. A shiver trickles down my spine.

That's the word for it. It is deeply unsettling, this place.

Kanuz seems unaffected by it, though. In fact, while I scrub at my skin and hum under my breath to break up the sound of the frustrated dinosaurs still bugling randomly outside and soak in the bizarre, otherworldly atmosphere, Kanuz just watches me with those strange, compelling eyes.

"Do your people mind the wet at all?" I've barely asked about him this whole time, preferring to stew over how sideways everything went and my fear for the rest of the crew.

He shakes his head, muttering something and pointing to the sky.

"Rains a little much here for that, huh?"

He nods, grinning at me with those too-sharp teeth. His smile sends a ripple of renewed interest through me.

That's unsettling, too.

I sigh, closing my eyes and floating, relaxed for the first time since we landed on this planet. I'm hungry, I'm tired, but I'm safe for the minute and I'm relatively clean.

And I am not going to psychoanalyze my growing attraction to the big, scaly alien. Nope. Not gonna do it.

I'm going to ignore it until the last possible minute.

"So, do you think I'll ever get back to Earth?" It's the first time I've put words to that particular worry.

Kanuz says nothing. Instead, a snarl rips out of him, and the next minute, water sloshes up the sides of my face as he storms from the pool.

Surprised, I flip right-side up, treading the lukewarm water and staring after Kanuz, whose tail thrashes behind him as he paces beside the pool, muttering to himself and stealing glances at me.

"What crawled up your butt?" I ask, annoyed at his quick change in behavior. "I thought we were finally getting along."

He raises a fist, pointing up at the… ceiling? The sky?

Unclear.

"I'm fucking sick of charades," I say, swimming for the edge of the pool. "You're mad at the rain?"

He grunts, kicking at a rock on the ground.

"That's a no. Okay, okay, lemme guess, three words, first word pissed, second word off, third word, alien." I laugh at my stupid joke, though it's not funny at all. Niki always says that humor is my crutch to avoid real feelings, and she's not wrong.

Doesn't mean I'm gonna change. Why mess with a good thing?

Kanuz points at me, the gesture so aggressive I flinch back, which only causes him to growl. He walks the length of the pool, then turns and walks back.

My translator spits out pure nonsense, as usual. "How can she not know? We are to live as one, and she does not know? How can it be that she desires to return to her village home life?"

I shake my head, my stomach sinking. Most of that actually made sense.

Which is *very* concerning. *Extremely* concerning.

What the hell is it that I don't know that's upsetting him so badly?

I dunk my slime-covered pants in the water. Why tackle an upset alien head-on when I can take care of the more immediate problem of wearing disgusting clothes? Absolutely no reason at all!

Still, it's troubling. He's clearly aggravated, and I know it has something to do with what I said about returning home.

It doesn't bode well.

I wash and wring out the clothes as best I can, the thick mud and slime sucked down into whatever drain must be in the bottom of the pool, leaving the rest pristine.

"Why is this place here? How in the world does this still function?" It's a marvel, and I stand up, my sodden clothes in hand. Water streams from my clothes as I wring them out, finally tugging them on, not quite brave enough to hang out in this freaky place in my underwear.

Boots are a good idea, and I go sockless, knowing all too well how much wet socks can fuck your world up. Trench foot would be a decidedly hellish development.

Kanuz is still fretting over whatever it is I don't know, but I studiously ignore him.

There's *plenty* I don't know. A metric fuckton, in fact. Especially about this planet, which has been shrouded in secrecy thanks to their sacred language and their interplanetary defense tech. My crew basically came in blind.

And look how great that turned out!

At this point, I'm not sure I *want* to know what missing information has him so upset.

Instead, I run a hand over the rough stone wall. It's smooth in some places, with swooping divots and dips. There's a thin layer of dust and dirt over everything, and when I clap my hands together, it clouds the air in front of me.

Coughing, my eyebrows raise as I study the wall.

It's not rough, not at all.

It's *carved*.

Every inch of it, thick with inscriptions in what I can only assume is the Suevan language. There are images, too, and a sense of wonder fills me as I drink it in. They're vaguely reminiscent of hieroglyphics—or maybe cuneiform—I studied what seems like a lifetime ago, but more pictorial than either of those systems.

I run my finger in the beveled edge of one, tracing the curve of a sinuous shape.

"What is this place?" Fear threads through my voice, because the longer I look at the wall, the longer the shapes start to mean something, which is… impossible. It should be *impossible*.

Two T-Rexes fighting a ridiculously huge snake should *also* be impossible, but I sure as shit watched that happen. Impossible, it seems, is a frame of mind. I snort, and then cough as I choke on more dust.

The images aren't friendly ones. No, not at all. There's the snake, which seems to be a theme of this swamp-ass planet, but it's not eating the friendly neighborhood dinosaur.

No. It's eating something with arms and legs and a Suevan shaped body.

Fuuuck.

"Kanuz," I say, quiet dread flooding me. Water drips from my hair to the floor, loud in his sudden silence. "Where did you take us?"

"Wife, do not touch anything here," Kanuz says. "There are many signs and statues, look at all the letters!"

I sigh in annoyance and frustration. Stupid translator.

"Why is this snake eating people?" I ask him, knowing I'm not going to get an answer. One I understand, in any case. I continue to rub away the accumulation of dirt and dust, stepping carefully around the random debris.

The carvings continue beneath a thick vine, and I tug at it, curious about what the hell this place is. The vine falls away easily under my hand, releasing an herbal fragrance as it gives way. It's a big improvement on the smell of the swamp. Massive. Huge. I inhale deeply, trying to resuscitate my sense of smell. Olfactory CPR.

Kanuz crowds behind me, so close the heat from his body warms my bare back. I expected him to be cool to the touch, at first, like a reptile. But he's not, he's warmer even than me, a fact I haven't taken for granted when the nights turn cold. "This is not human place, snake worship eat chicken."

"Thanks," I say. "Great."

I'd much rather think about what the story is behind this temple than chase the same depressing thoughts like a hamster on a wheel.

A snake statue protrudes from the wall, dipping in and out of it. Here, the wall is carved to resemble a pool of water, rippling around where the body of the stone snake disappears into it.

"Oh, *wow*." Each scale is so neatly articulated, and as I run my fingers over it, the grime gives way to something polished and shining. It's not stone at all, but some kind of gem.

"This is gorgeous." A thrill goes through me at finding something so unexpectedly beautiful. As I scrub the dust and leaf debris away, a deep, shimmering purple is revealed, each scale carved so carefully it almost seems real. "Not real sure I can get down with the giant snake worship or whatever you have going on here, but this is cool all the same."

The exasperated sound Kanuz makes is so human, I can't help but snort as I glance over my shoulder at him. His long thick hair's braided back, and it drips wet across his chest, where it glistens as it runs down the deep furrows of his insanely ripped abs.

I have *got* to stop ogling his bod. Kanuz is not an alien object of worship, unlike the purple snake under my fingers.

Oh god. Purple snake. No doubt Bex, the resident monster-fucker reader on our crew, would have some thoughts about that. I stifle a laugh, biting my cheeks in a lackluster attempt to keep it in.

"So, uh, Kanuz, the snake here, this big, thick, purple snake… it's not, like, a symbol for something else, is it? Like, does it mean something?"

What would Bex say? This time the laugh erupts out of me, and it feels so good to imagine what the over-the-top tech specialist would say about finding a big, ridged purple snake in the alien jungle that it nearly eclipses the overwhelming worry that chases the thought.

My laughter dies quickly at the thought, and I sober, gnawing at my lower lip.

I hope they're all right. I hope that Niki and the other six of our crew aren't being terrorized by dinosaurs. Fuck. I even hope

Dox io living her monster fucker dream and getting it on with the locals.

Better than the alternative, that they're—

I take a deep breath and refuse to let myself even think it.

The carved snake's head juts from the wall ahead, and I continue running my fingers along the sinuous body, stepping over a tree root to get a better look at the work of art that's the head.

"Holy hell," I breathe, rubbing the polished orb of the eye. "Is this… a diamond?" Under the smooth exterior, the eye's been cut into a million fractured facets, and as I wipe away the dirt crusting it, it catches the light from the opening in the roof.

A brilliant prism flashes across the temple, a hundred tiny rainbows suddenly cutting through the gloom of the ruin. A shiver runs down my spine. The effect is breath-taking and eerie all at once.

"Wow," I say. "And here I was, thinking the roof just fell in. It already had a hole in it, didn't it?"

"Time is not a forgiving entity, even for mother Sueva," Kanuz says.

I tug at my ear lobe. "You know, that almost made sense." I peer up at him in surprise, my fingers still rubbing the surface of the eye of the snake.

It depresses under my fingers, and a loud click reverberates off the stone.

"Oh, shit," I say. Did I break it? Stupid, stupid, stupid—

The ground rumbles under my feet, a horrible grating noise sounding. Leaves fall to the floor from the tree that's taken up residence in the ruin.

"Is it an earthquake?" I yell, my eyes wide. I brace my feet, trying to remain upright. "Sueva quake?"

That's just what I need, for a fucking earthquake to take me out.

No sooner has the thought flashed through my mind than the floor gives way under my feet.

I'm so shocked I can't even scream. A strong, taloned hand grips my bicep, and Kanuz yanks me against him.

Then I'm free-falling, cocooned between his scaled chest and tree-trunk like arms.

CHAPTER
SIX

KANUZ

THIS IS GOING TO HURT.

Still, I would much rather bear the brunt of the fall than allow my mate to absorb the impact with her soft human flesh. I barely know the female, and yet I find the thought of any injury to her body completely abhorrent.

I refuse to let it happen, so I cradle her to me. Her body is tense with terror at first, a normal reaction to falling suddenly, but then she goes loose and soft against me.

Good. It will be better if she's fainted.

"Fuck," she says, and surprise widens my eyes. "This is gonna be bad enough without whiplash."

Brilliant female.

The ground slams into us. Pain jolts up my tail at the impact. Water splashes in the dark, and then we're sinking fast.

It was a trap door. It wasn't ground at all, but another flowing pool. My relief is short-lived, my need to get out of the water and breathe warring with the worry of what else might be in this pool —in this ruined temple.

There is no telling.

With one arm around Gen's chest, I kick, and for a horror filled moment, I pray to the mother goddess that the direction I've blindly chosen is indeed up, and that I'm not driving us further into the deep water.

Finally, air breaks around us, and Gen gasps, then coughs, wriggling against me like a caught fish. "What the fuck was that?"

"Trap door," I say automatically. I tread water with her pressed against me, and my body responds to her nearness, the adrenaline melting way to something much more pleasurable.

"Trap door?" she repeats.

Exhilaration courses through me, despite the seriousness of our latest dangerous predicament.

"Did you understand me?" I begin swimming, carrying her on top of me, knowing that the edge of this underground pool is somewhere around us. The ancients did not construct their puzzle boxes of worship as death traps. Well, not *all* of them, at the very least.

I send up another quick prayer that this temple is *not* one of those. But the goddess is called many-faced for a reason, and it is just as likely this temple pays respects to one of her more violent aspects as it is to be dedicated to a motherly one.

With all the violent imagery on the walls above, the latter is much less likely.

"You said trap door?" she asks, her body tense once more. "I thought this place was a temple. A ruin. How the hell can there *still* be a functioning trap door? Not to mention, why would they even put one in a *temple*?"

"I cannot believe you understand me now, my flower. I have so much to tell you."

She tugs at her earlobe. "I mean, I can mostly understand you, but I'm not sure why you're calling me a flower. My name is Gen. Genevieve. Maybe that doesn't translate. Is Gen a type a flower here?"

"It is now," I tell her earnestly.

"Huh. Still some kinks to work out, I guess. What kind of translator is this anyway? It reminds me a little of the time Den tried to bore me to death explaining machine learning and AI. From what I understood of it anyway." Her voice trails off, contemplative.

Truly, I cannot believe how this female accepts things. Any of the other alien species I've taken to bed would have been screaming or crying now at being tossed into a dark, water filled pit, not to mention the Crigomar attack.

Gen simply soldiers on, tougher than many Suevan warriors I've fought beside. She will make a fine queen of my planet one day.

My quickly inflating pride bursts at the thought, replaced by self-loathing. If the separatists can be brought to heel, that is. Because at this point, if I do not figure out a solution to my planet's political troubles, all I've won for Gen will be war and strife.

Maybe my father is right. Maybe I am not strong enough to rule. A low growl rips out of me, and Gen's body goes taut against mine.

"What is it, Kanuz? Fuck, I wish I had my gun. Stupid diplomatic protocols."

"We will find you a weapon," I tell her. What I will find for her, I do not know. Another false promise. Another reason I'm not enough for the Suevans to unite behind.

"You will find me a big stick?" she replies, confusion lacing her tone.

I cannot help the chuckle that comes out of me. "Big stick? Is that what your translator says? When we reach my hometown of Perzivor, I will be having a long talk with our scientists about making improvements to this technology."

It makes sense though, that they wouldn't work correctly right away, considering we hold the secrets of our native tongue closely, the sacred truth-telling words something we do not share freely with other species.

Now though? Now, I wish we had spent more time on improving the symbiont that my entire world hinges on. Because, if I do not have my people united, I will have my Gen. And now that my wife can understand me, our quandary does not seem so very terrible.

Finally, my feet touch solid ground, and I heave a sigh of relief. "We're at the shoreline." I swing her up into my arms, the chamber we've fallen into so pitch black I can hardly make out her features, even with my excellent eyesight.

"Can you see in the dark?" I ask her, unsure about human vision.

"I wish," she snorts. "No, I'm more than happy to have you use your big muscles and carry me around. The last thing I need is a broken leg. I'm not too proud to realize *that*."

"Do not even joke about it," I tell her. I flex my muscles, pleased she's noticed their size. "I would not have any of your petals crushed, my flower."

"Damn, just when I think this translator thing is working, it spits out the most random shit." Her tone is resigned. "Unless you are, in fact, calling me a flower."

"Why would I not call you a flower?" I ask. The water laps around my thighs now, and a shiver wracks Gen's body. "You are the most stunning creature I have ever seen," I tell her earnestly. It is true, too. "As Prince of Sueva, I have had my choice of consorts. All kinds of species, all considered beautiful. You eclipse them all, and I am truly proud to have selected you as my wife."

She clears her throat, her fingers gripping my forearm more tightly. "I'm sorry, *what*?"

"I have tasted the delights of females from across the galaxy, but your nectar is all that interests me now, my flower."

"My *what*?!"

I frown, irritated that the translator seems to be malfunctioning again. "Your honey. Your nectar. The juices of your pleasure. The sweetness between your legs."

"What the fuck?" she whispers. I can barely see her face, but her eyes are wide and shining. She squirms against my grip, pushing against me.

I loose a low growl. "Do you want me to put you down and chase you? Is this the way of mated humans, my sweet wife? You enjoy the chase?"

"Wait. Wait." She pushes her hand against my face.

Perhaps she wants me to lick it. Humans are strange. I press my tongue against her palm, and she lets out a small squeal of surprise.

"Stop," she says. "Put me down."

Confused, I do as she asks. In the dark, I can see her place her hands on her hips, a stern expression on her face at odds with the delectable scent of her arousal.

"I can smell you are ready to mate," I tell her.

"Why… Why would you—" She holds up a hand. "You know what? I don't want to know. What I want you to do, my fine scaled friend, is get us the hell out of here." Gen plunks down on the ground, the water licking around her boots. She takes them off, dumping the liquid that's pooled there out. A small fish wiggles free of one, but she appears not to notice.

I boggle at her, turning her words over in my head.

"What do you mean, you do not *want* to know? You do not want me to tell you of how I will bury my head between your legs and wring screams of pleasure from you?"

"Did you not just tell me all about how many other women you've had sex with? That's not the compliment you think it is, my dude."

"I do not know what this dude is you speak of. If that is what you want me to be to you, I will be it. And why would that not please you? I have practiced until I am very skilled with many kinds of females. I have never known a human female, but I am confident in my ability to lick your cunt."

The perfume of her mating scent grows stronger. I smile to myself, my tail lashing behind me.

"A dude is just a word. A saying. Uh, kinda like friend. And I am not saying, ah, what you're suggesting is a complete no," she says thickly, "but we have several things we should discuss first, and I'm not doing any of that in the dark, in a ruined temple, with dinosaurs and prehistoric snake monsters lurking about." A small laugh erupts from her. "Snake monsters."

She mutters something about a one-eyed purple monster under her breath.

Disappointed but determined to do as she asks, I trudge up the gravelly shore, wracking my memory of what I was taught years ago about the ancients. There should be a light source around here. A glassy-textured wall looms before me, reflecting the dark and my own silhouette.

I trace the tips of my talons over it, searching for a clue as to what will illuminate the space. The ancients wanted their peers and heirs to marvel at their creations, trap doors and all. There will be a way to light this pit, I only have to find it.

"Do not worry, my wife, my sweet flower, I will find a way to bring light to this place, and then I will look upon you as you scream my name in hedonistic desire."

"Wife?" Gen asks loudly from behind me, a note of something unfathomable in her voice. "Wife. What the *fuck*? I thought that was a translation fail. The fuck?!"

"We will," I agree, pleased she's decided to succumb to my mating overtures already. "You will be a treasured princess among my people once I am able to rescue you from this situation we find ourselves in."

"Princess?" she asks, a weary note to her voice. "Is this like the flower thing? A cute name for your pet human? Can you just call me Gen? I'm trying to roll with the punches here, my dude, because frankly, there's not a whole lot of other options available, but call me Gen."

"Princess Gen of Sueva, the Light of Perzivor," I agree. "My bride and chosen, my human flower."

"Fuck." Then, a beat later, "You're a prince. And you're telling me we're married." Her voice is flat, and I turn away from the wall and my search, frowning into the darkness at her.

"Of course, we are married. That is what happens after a mating ceremony, after all. You chose to come here as our brides, a token of good-will from your Earth Federation in exchange for our technology. Was our communication unclear?" I chuckle at her obvious joke. "You ate from my hand, I ate from yours, you danced with me. We are wed. Now you are a princess of the Suevan people, and I—"

I stop talking, familiar shame filling me as she remains silent, the only sound the gentle lapping of water against the shore and her sharp, uneven breathing.

"You did not know?"

"No, my dude, *Prince* of Sueva, I most decidedly did not know. The Federation left that tiny piece of information out of our mission briefing. Did Niki know? She couldn't have known. She would have told me. I'll kill her if she knew."

"I find your bloodthirstiness most alluring," I tell her, my cock rising immediately.

"That's messed up," she says, "but thanks, I guess."

"Would you like to appreciate it with your hand?"

"Can you not? Now is not the time," she sputters, and I frown.

"So there *will* be a time?" I cannot keep the hope out of my voice, and sudden wonder fills me. Have I ever been as besotted with a female? Is it because she is mine, my mate, and I long to claim her as the goddess demands?

A weary sigh sounds. "I tell you what, buddy. If you can get us out of this pit, I will blow your damn mind."

"My dam mind?" She would seek to let the tide of my passions loose, surging forth from a burst dam? I was already motivated to find a safe exit for us, but now? Now I would move the skies themselves for a chance at what she has promised.

She is my wife, and I will enjoy every morsel she deigns to give me.

Finally, my talons scrabble over a familiar surface, one every

Suevan worth his quarn knows as soon as he can stand. A smug smile curls my lips, and I strike my talons across the rougher surface of the wall. Sparks fly and briefly illuminate Gen's enticing figure, before igniting the tinder inlaid inside the wall. A line of fire rapidly consumes it, racing along the glossy surface. I blink against the sudden light.

"Did you light that fire with your *fingers*?" The firelight flickers across her stunned features, and she trudges closer to the wall, wet and shivering slightly.

"How else would I have done it? Do human males not know how to do this?"

"They probably couldn't find the spot to hit if they wanted to." She laughs at this, and I frown, confused.

"You think it is funny that your males do not know how to make fire?"

Gen doubles over, and alarm fills me, until a hoarse wheezing noise chokes out of her. When she straightens up, her eyes leak and her shoulders shake. With laughter.

"Oh," she finally gasps. "Don't worry, we'll just pretend they did."

"Wife, why do I feel as though there is something to this joke that I do not understand?"

Her laughter dies as quickly as it started, and I narrow my eyes, concerned about her rapid change in mood.

"Please… just don't. Call me Gen. Not… not the other."

Her hair glows gold in the firelight. Disappointment winds through me, tightening my scales and making my tail lash errati-cally. "Are you so displeased about it?"

"Are you fucking *kidding* me?" She gapes at me for a moment, her mouth opening and closing like a fish. "I didn't *know* I was marrying you. None of us knew. It has nothing to do with *you*, so don't go getting all weird." Anger flits across her face, chased off by sullen resignation.

"So you would choose me as I chose you?" It pleases me to think that out of all the warlords, she would pick me, the 'spoiled' prince of Sueva. My molars grind together, and one of my fangs pricks against my lower lip.

She pinches the bridge of her nose, sighing deeply. "Kanuz. Can you focus on getting us out of here? That would make me want to choose you."

"You promised to blow my dam when we leave. Do not think I won't remember."

"What?" Her jaw drops open, her eyes wide with surprise. "Blow your dam? Oh, god, you mean when I said I'd blow your mind..." She starts laughing again.

"I will *remember*." Annoyed and amused by her giggles, I turn back to the wall. Everything the Suevan priestesses taught me about the ancients and their temples says the key to getting out of this trap lies somewhere on this glossy wall.

"What are all these markings? Is it a language? This is different from the hieroglyphs with the snake statue."

"It's ancient Suevan." I cross my arms, standing back and picking out a few choice phrases. "I learned it from the priestesses charged with my education at a young age, but it has been many, many years."

"They teach everyone ancient dead languages?"

"There is no such thing as a dead language," I tell her, confused. "If it has been spoken, if there are still records of it, then it is still alive, is it not? How could a language die?"

"I just meant, since no one speaks it anymore—"

"The ancients still speak it," I tell her, pointing to the wall. "Do you not see their words written here, same as I do?"

"Right. Sure. Okay, fine. Not a *dead* language. So then, Mr. Smarty-pants, what does it say?"

I gawk at her, the ancient Suevan melting from my mind as I try to make sense of her words. "Why do you think my pants are smart? Do you find them attractive? I can promise you, they will look better off than on, if only you—"

"Stop." She holds up a hand, but her lips are curved in a smirk, a small laugh erupting out of her again. "Can you focus?"

"It is very hard to focus when you are near, Gen. But I will do as you wish."

I squat next to the first string of words, squinting at the text etched in the tablet wall. A strange rattling sounds behind me, but I ignore it, focused on doing what my stubborn mate insists.

I would like her to blow my dam very much indeed.

CHAPTER
SEVEN

GEN

I STRETCH my hands out toward the fire that burns in a strange spiral on the wall, casting odd shadows. It's weird as fuck, but it's hot. And right now? Hot is all I care about. After our impromptu dip in the ice-cold pool, I need all the warmth I can get.

And I need to figure out what the fuck I'm going to do about my new *husband*. I always knew the Federation was squirrely as all hell, and my constant disagreement and butting heads with the top brass is one of the reasons I've been stuck as first officer instead of moving up the ranks.

Still.

Marrying us off to aliens as a price for tech?

That's some fucked up shit, even for the Federation.

I cross my arms over my chest, grinding my teeth together to keep them from chattering. I haven't had enough calories today, and I can't afford to expend much more energy. I creep closer to the fire, watching Kanuz.

The Prince of Sueva.

My *husband*.

Making me, Genevieve Durand, the princess of this alien

planet. I don't know whether to laugh or scream, so a weird, choked noise comes out of me instead, my teeth rattling against each other as a shiver wracks me.

The heat from the fire in the wall seeps through my clothes, and I'm grateful that Kanuz is, at the very least, not a Roth.

The enemy of my enemy is my husband, I guess.

I might come off like a blunt asshole most of the time, another fact that's kept me from moving up the ranks and likely why the Federation jumped at the chance to throw me to the Suevans, but I'm also a realist.

The reality here is twofold:

Firstly, I have myself an alien husband. As far as aliens go, I could be much, much worse off. Kanuz is… hot. Like, super buff. For a human, that kind of musculature would be impossible, and I like sex and men too much not to appreciate it. His face is handsome, even by human standards, though his features are sharper and more rugged than any human I've ever seen.

Heat runs through me, despite the soaked clothes and my dripping hair.

Secondly, I need him. I'm stuck in an alien jungle with no weapons, no knowledge of this place, and he's kept me alive pretty much single-handedly.

It should irk me. Usually, it would.

It's a sign of how fucking exhausted I am that I can't muster up more than gratitude and relief that he's on my side.

At least he's not a Roth.

I peel off my sodden tank, wringing it out, yet again.

At least, I'm clean.

At least, I can *finally* fucking talk to him. The amount of relief the thought gives me has me sagging as the weight lifts. I may have had him as a companion for the last week and half, but not being able to communicate has made this week a lonely hell.

"Why human women?" There are hundreds of alien species out there, and that's just the ones Earth knows about.

Kanuz huffs out a breath, turning to glance at me over his

shoulder before facing the wall again. "Because you can bear our children."

My stomach flips. Maybe I shouldn't have asked. "Bear your children? Babies? Why can't you do that with your own people?"

"There are no Suevan women, not anymore."

"But there were Suevan women at the welcoming," I choke. "Marriage ceremony."

"They are elders. There have been no females born in generations."

"Babies," I say again, light-headed. "You want to breed us."

"My wife, if you keep speaking of breeding, I will not be able to control myself. Your beauty already tempts me beyond all reason." His voice is a low, husky growl, and the promise in his words sends a thrill through me.

Which it absolutely shouldn't! Sure, I can't help feeling slightly delighted by his obvious fascination with me, but…

I don't want babies.

Well, that's not entirely true. My mouth twists to the side, and I scooch as close as I dare to the flaming wall. I've always wanted a family, always wanted little sassy kids and fat toddlers to squish.

Until the Roth came and destroyed that dream, just like they destroyed so much of Earth.

"My mate," Kanuz says, "I can smell your arousal."

"You can do *what* now?!"

"Does the thought of me rutting you and making you swell arouse you as much as it does me? Your body tells me it does."

"You can smell me?" I don't even know what to do with that information. Frankly, we went from zero to sixty on the communication scale. Sixty is a little too fast.

And I should not be thinking about sixty-nine.

"Your scent is the most delectable thing I have ever experienced." His diamond pupils expand as he watches me from over his shoulder, his translations forgotten. "Say the word, and I will gladly bury myself in your eager cunt."

"Whoa," I say, my eyes wide. "Listen buddy, I've had my share of dirty talking partners in bed, but I can't say anyone's ever told me that." And I've always loved dirty talk, and even now, knowing that this alien wants to get me pregnant, that that's why he married me… I'm turned on.

This is… a lot.

He stands up, towering over me, and I swallow hard. "Do you want that, my flower?"

My stomach growls, and I blink, the spell of attraction suddenly snapped.

Kanuz's lip curls, disgust clear on his green features. His tail whips behind him, and he mutters something to himself before turning back to the wall.

I sink to the floor, crossing my legs and putting my face in my hands. What am I doing? Am I seriously thinking about fucking this massive alien?

Yeah, yeah I am. Yep.

Maybe it's a combination of dehydration and hunger and exposure.

Or maybe I *want* him. Maybe I, the most stubborn, meanest person I know, likes the idea of someone else shouldering some of the burden for a while. Of being protected by a huge dude.

Of not having to worry about when the Roth will attack again, because I'll be *here*, away from the reality of their assault.

Or maybe I'm losing my mind. A memory of the Roth attack surfaces, and bile fills my throat, my pulse quickening. The smell of burning buildings, so many on fire that the sky rained ash for a day after. The sound of screams. The frenzied run from Houston down highways packed tight with cars that would be incinerated by the Roth in the coming hours.

"I was right," he says suddenly, and I flinch, slamming the door to those memories shut.

"About what?"

"This temple. This is no ordinary temple." His voice is full of excitement, the words tumbling over each other.

"Is that a good thing? Does that mean we can get out more easily?"

"It is the best thing, my human flower."

"That sounds… gross. Don't call me that."

He frowns at me, then beams, flashing fangs in a boyish grin that's so charming I can't help but smile back a little. "What would you have me call you, then? My starlight? My soft moonbeam? My little mate? Tell me, so that when I bury my cock inside you, I know what you want to hear me moan."

"Gen is fine," I croak, face heating. "Let's just get out of here before we worry about that."

"No, I will think of something perfect for you, my Gen." He steps closer, his chest brushing against my breasts. "I will be the only one to call you this name, so that when you hear it, you perfume the air with the scent of your arousal, and I'll know you long to have me inside you."

"For crying out loud." I scrub a hand over my face. "Just tell me what the damn wall says."

"Dam wall? No, it is just a regular wall. There is no water behind it."

Ugh.

"This is the temple of the snake goddess. One of the many faces of the mother goddess."

"Ooookay," I say slowly. "Tell me more."

"This is the temple where the true treasure of Sueva is hidden."

"Is that treasure food?" I say, arching a brow at him. "Because we can't eat treasure, and your wife is hungry."

"Hungry for food or cock?" he says, smirking at me. "I can still scent you."

"Fucking hell," I say, shoving him away from me. "For food."

"Food will not be a problem." His eyes shine in the firelight, his third eyelid blinking open and shut as he stares at me. "The pool behind us is full of fish and fresh water. It's filtered, too. I could feel it pulling on my toes as I swam with you soft in my arms."

"So we're safe in here." I narrow my eyes at him. There's something he's not telling me. "Because treasure doesn't fucking matter if we die trying to get it."

"Eh," he says, shrugging. "We are no worse off than we would be in the jungle with the separatists and Crigomar after us."

"Separatists… That's why we're in the jungle?" I have vague memories of an explosion, of blinding pain, before I woke up in a downpour with Kanuz's worried mug swimming overhead. "They attacked the welcoming ceremony."

"Marriage ceremony," Kanuz corrects, and I blow out an irritated breath. "But yes."

"They would attack the prince?"

"They have many reasons to despise me, but the most important of them is that they do not approve of our choice to blend our species, even if it means the survival of Suevans. They believe the mother goddess disapproves, too." His tail smashes against the stone wall, his expression tight with displeasure.

"Riiiight. So… I'm not safe here, then." Fuck. Talk about bursting my bubble. He *skewered* it.

"I will keep you safe, my flower. I will keep you safe, and happy, and treasure your every breath. You are the most enchanting female I have ever seen. I like your spikes as well."

"My spikes?" I say, confusion overriding my many questions.

"You are angry and mean, and I find it most charming."

"Oh," I say. That's a new one.

"The treasure of this temple is not like most," Kanuz says, his eyes alight with sudden zeal. It's infectious, and a little thrill of excitement goes through me. "This treasure could reunite Sueva under my rule."

"What is it?" I ask, interested despite myself. If the way to treasure is just as dangerous as a jungle full of angry Suevans and dinosaurs, then maybe I should take my chances on it. Why not?

It's not like I have anything left to lose, anyway. Go big or go home.

Or, you know, *never* go home. Whatever.

I snort.

"It is the symbol of the many-faced-goddess herself. A symbol that will reunite all of Sueva. No one would contest my rule if I had it in my possession." A muscle ticks in his forehead.

"What is it? Gems? A crown? A scepter? Some kind of technology?"

He shakes his head, a crazed look in his eye. "That is the best part, my cunning diamond. I do not know."

"Cunning diamond?" I scowl at him, then shake off his new weird nickname. "How is *that* the best part? How would your people even know it's supposed to reunite them? Isn't that the whole point of a symbol? That people recognize it?"

"That doesn't make any sense." He gapes at me, his head tilted to the side. "The mysterious nature of the symbol is the important part."

I can't help but roll my eyes. "You're literally making no sense."

"You dare tell a prince of Sueva such a thing?"

"Yeah, absolutely, you big idiot," I say, annoyed beyond reason. Hangry and cold do not my best moments make, but I can't stop myself. I poke him straight in the chest. "While I am not *opposed* to a treasure hunt—because from the looks of it, we're stuck in here unless you can figure out a way to get us out of a hole fifty feet up—and I'm all about *why not?* adventures, I fail to see the logic of a symbol *nobody* recognizes."

"What you fail to see, my angry flower, is that the symbol will be instantly recognizable. What the symbol is, however, is a mystery, so that only the worthy may find it." He takes my fisted hand from where it presses against his chest. His hands are so big his talons curl all the way around mine. Slowly, fire blazing in his eyes, he brings my hand to his lips, and when he kisses the top slowly, sensuously, desire rushes through me. "I like when you are like this. I like when you are testy and challenging and that you do not care about my title."

"I only just found out about your title, so don't get any ideas," I grump at him, my irritability headed off by his surprising kiss. I yank my hand away, much too late to have any real meaning.

"You can pretend all you want, my mean little flower, but I can scent how you really feel."

"I honestly don't know how to feel about that," I tell him, amused by his tenacity in spite of myself.

"You like it," he tells me, his lips curling back in a wide smile. "And you will agree to find this treasure with me, because I can tell you like the idea, and while we hunt for this treasure, you will slowly succumb to my lust for you. When we leave this temple with the blessing of the many faced-goddess, you will be swelling with my child and all of Sueva will bow at your feet."

"That's a whole lot of talk, Prince," I say, scowling at him. "You know what they say about people who make assumptions."

"I'm a prince, as you so rightly remembered. I don't make assumptions. I make the rules." His grin is so cocky and self-satis-fied that I can't help laughing again. "I like that sound, my princess, my flower."

"Gen," I say, rolling my eyes again.

"I cannot wait to learn every sound that those pretty red lips make, my Gen." Kanuz leans close, brushing his mouth over my forehead.

I step backward, trying to gather my scattered wits about me. This alien is irrepressible. He might be more stubborn and cocky than me, and that's saying something.

"I like this game," he says suddenly, licking his lips.

"I'm not playing a game," I say.

"You are. You act like you do not want me, but your body tells the truth. It will be very fun when I finally have my way with you, Princess."

"Don't call me princess. Just call me Gen." A tiny thrill goes through me, though. This alien would hand me safety. A crown. His attention, which I find more and more that I don't mind.

A family.

"See?" he says, eyeing me with amusement. "Your little fights are such fun."

"Well, you better catch me some fish or show me how to, because your little flower is fucking hungry."

"I never thought I'd want a female who was so bossy and stubborn. But I find that I quite like this. My cock has never been so hard. My xof already sings for you."

I stare at him, my translator giving me nothing for that word. "I can't with you."

"You can and you will," he says cheerily. "And you will blow my dam."

With that, he pulls his leather-like pants down, and my jaw drops.

He's hard and huge. Huge, hard, and... weird. Not bad weird, just... not-human weird. His dick is covered in smooth, scale-like bumps, and like the rest of him, is a shade of green. A small nub sits above his dick, and as I stare, it vibrates, just slightly.

My insides clench on nothing. I can't look away.

"You like it already," he crows, pleased at my reaction.

"It looks like a sex toy," I say, finally tearing my gaze away. "That looks..." I bite off my observation. Because as much fun as his downtown cityscape seems, it wouldn't be just an amusement park.

Nah.

It would mean babies.

Alien babies.

His cock would already be a lot to take in. I'm not sure about the whole package it comes with.

Still, I have an IUD. Maybe I could take him for a whirl without any alien spawn. What would our baby even look like? I squeeze my eyes shut, banishing the thought.

I thought I gave up that dream, the idea of a family. It's too much now to even consider it. Too painful. I know all too well how much hope can hurt. It's easier to ask *why not* instead of *why*. It's easier to push people away. To be prickly and keep everyone at arm's length.

Kanuz walks into the depths of the clear pool, sparkling with the firelight. He sinks deeper and deeper into the water, his tail lashing behind him and propelling him forward.

He has a tail. A tail!

I can't really be thinking about having sex with him, can I?

Why not?

CHAPTER
EIGHT

KANUZ

GEN OCCUPIES NEARLY ALL my thoughts. I cannot seem to stop about the way her ample breasts heaved as she stared up at me, about the feel of her soft skin against my lips, her brow furrowed in consternation.

Cool water sluices around me, and I surge through it, aiming deep, where I know the fish keep to the dark recesses. Sure enough, the white scales flash in the darkness, but I strike before it can swim away, my talons spearing it. I give a mighty kick and launch myself towards the surface.

Gen will be pleased. I am pleased. These fish are a delicacy, the white flesh tender and delicious. From the looks of it, there are plenty to feast on while we search for the many-faced goddess' treasure.

Air bursts around me as I reach the surface, and I draw in a great lungful, the fish squirming fruitlessly against my hold on it.

"That was fast," Gen says, and there's a note of appreciation in her voice.

Pride fills me. "I am a good provider and protector."

"And so humble," she says, but a hint of a smile offsets the biting sarcasm in her voice.

"A prince has no need to be humble. I was raised to rule, not raised to meekly follow. I was raised for command." I stride from the pool, water streaming down my naked body, and I notice as Gen's gaze dips to where my cock stands proudly between my legs. "Look your fill," I purr, "soon I will be the one filling you."

She snorts, raising one eyebrow before examining the fish in my hand.

She does not contradict me, however, and for that alone, triumph fills me.

My wife is considering it—taking me fully as her husband. I cannot wait to complete our mating, even though a small part of me still hears my father's voice in my head.

That I am not ready for the crown, ready for rule. That I am not enough for Sueva.

How can I be enough for this feisty human female, a leader amongst her people?

I give my head a little shake, as though that will shake loose the negative thoughts rooted deep in my brain.

I don't want them there. I want *her* there, I want her to fill my thoughts, her light banishing the darkness threatening there. I want to lose myself in her completely.

She's a dangerous thing, this human female.

"You're looking at me strangely," she says, her adorable nose wrinkled, her hair drying in golden waves across her shoulders.

"I want you," I tell her simply. There's no need to pretend otherwise. I've never had to work this hard for a female, and this one is already wed to me.

"Food," she says, carefully enunciating the word. "Tell me how to eat this thing."

"You've never had fish before? Do they not have fish on your planet?"

"I've had fish. Do you eat it whole? Raw?"

I squint at her. "Are you joking? Do humans eat it whole and raw?"

"Uh, sometimes we eat it raw. It's called sushi."

"If you would like to eat it raw, my flower, that is up to you. I would recommend using the fire to cook it, though."

"Right." She stares at the fish in my hands.

"Here, my prickly flower, sit and I will serve you."

She grumbles something under her breath that sounds suspiciously like an insult, and I laugh softly, slicing a talon through the soft flesh of the fish. "It has been a long while since I cleaned a fish, but I have many fond memories of my father, the king, taking me out when I was young. Before my mother died."

"Oh," Gen's face crumples, then smooths out. "I'm sorry to hear that, about your mother."

"The same virus that kept our species from producing females also caused many of them to die. My mother was one of many to suffer from it." It was awful at the end, watching her slowly waste away, in pain. It was nearly a relief when she finally succumbed to it. "I miss her every day," I tell Gen.

"My parents were killed in the Roth invasion. Niki's were too. Niki is our captain," she says quietly. "Most of us were orphaned that day. Mine were civilians, though—a lot of the women in our crew grew up military."

She goes silent, her eyes clouded with painful memories. I want to reach out and touch her, to offer her the small physical comfort, but since I'm currently eviscerating a fish, I refrain. I do not think she would like to be covered in fish muck.

"I am sorry for you, too. The Roth are a blight on the universe," I say instead. "There are rumors that the Roth are to blame for the virus."

"They killed hundreds of thousands of my people. They didn't need a virus. Just their superior weapons." She picks up a pebble from the floor, running her fingers over it. "I had to join up after what they did. Everything changed after that week."

"Why did they leave Earth?" It's a question we could never

figure out; why the Roth would invade and then abandon such a primitive planet, ripe for the picking.

"We repelled them. Not at first, obviously, but we destroyed enough of their ships that they left."

I frown, slicing the fish meat into bite size chunks. "That's not like them."

They should have sent more. It doesn't add up.

"Why didn't you help? If Sueva was concerned about the Roth, then why didn't you step up?"

I blink at her, surprised at her line of questioning. "We are helping now," I answer cautiously. "We are sending the interplanetary defense system your Federation asked for."

"Did you know they would attack Earth?"

"We were busy defending settlements on other planets. They are a vicious species." Memories churn through me, memories I'm certain she shares too. If not the exact same, then the same flavor of destruction, of blood and of pain.

"We have video of Suevans attacking Roth at your settlements. We had to reverse engineer their tech to get it, but their invasion advanced what we could do exponentially."

"That is good, for a primitive species."

She gawks at me for a minute. "Primitive? You're the one gutting that fish with your bare hands."

I hold the carcass out to her. "Would you prefer to do it?"

"With what?" She holds up her blunt fingers. "It's just—we're not… Okay. I guess we are—were—primitive."

"My prickly flower, could it be that you are agreeing with me?"

"No." She squints at me. "You really think we're primitive?"

"Did you Federation tell you the true purpose of your mission here?" I still can't quite wrap my head around their lies. "That you were to marry into our race for breeding purposes? You tell me that they did not allow you this choice, and in the next breath claim that your species is not the primitive one? We never imagined the females that came to us would not know the reason why." Anger rises in me, and I stand abruptly, leaving the fileted fish on the smooth stone.

Her lips purse, and she throws the pebble into the pool beyond, where it splashes against the surface. "You have a point."

"Ah, my sweet Gen, are you feeling feverish? You are agreeable. You must be famished indeed."

"Shut up," she grumbles, then snorts a tiny human laugh.

I smirk at her faux ire. The roots of the zitsu tree that's claimed this temple sprout several branches, and I trek over to where they are, snapping them off cleanly while Gen glowers at me from her curled up position near the warmth of the ancient's puzzle wall.

I may have oversold how easy it will be to solve the mystery of this place, but I am nothing if not confident in my ability to find this treasure. I must be, because only one who is worthy of the treasure will find it. Such is the way of the goddess.

The branches snap easily, and I send up a silent prayer of thanks as I walk back to my mate and our meal. Though I have never been truly religious, it seems best to err on the side of piety when searching for the goddess' treasure.

I skewer the meat on the green boughs, then singe it over the flame in the wall.

"How long will it last?"

"I assume we will eat some now and fish again after resting. Are you not hungry?"

"No, I mean the fire."

"It should burn for the next eight days or so, if I remember correctly, giving us enough time to find the treasure and find our way out of the maze."

"It's a maze?"

I sigh, handing her the first skewer full of meat. "It is like a puzzle box, this temple. There will be more traps and riddles, and likely dangers along the way."

"Like dinosaurs and giant snakes? Or… like angry aliens who want to murder me because *you* want to knock me up?"

Aghast, I stare at her, my own skewer of fish meat burning

where I hold it against the flame. "I would never hit you. Is this something men from your planet do? It is unthinkable to strike one's mate."

Her eyes go wide, and she shakes her head before laughing, the sound loud in the quiet of the temple, echoing off the hard surfaces. "No, no, that's not what I meant. Although, that's good, *good*. Yeah. No, it means to get pregnant."

My cock grows immediately hard again, and I groan with the need to slake my lust. "Do not speak of it unless you are ready to take me."

"Is it really that exciting for you? The thought of that?" Her brow quirks, and she bites into the meat. Her expression changes instantly as she chews, and the meat disappears into her pretty mouth. Satisfaction fills me. I did that. I provided for my female, and now she makes happy, contented noises as she chews.

"It is more than exciting," I tell her. "I can scent that you are ready to swell with my child."

"That's… ah, humans can't do that."

"Suevan women can only orgasm when they are ready to be mated, and your scent tells me that you are ready to be plea-sured." I chew my own fish, lust roaring through me as I watch her through heavy lids.

"Well, I can tell you this, my scaley dude, that is not true of humans. Not at all. We can come any time, any place, and orgasms aren't just for babies." She laughs, then eyes the rest of the fish. I take her empty skewer and refill it, charring the fish just so.

"You would not speak of your orgasms if you knew what it did to me, your dude."

When I hand it back to her, she's watching me with a careful, curious expression. "Thank you. For catching the fish and cooking it."

"Tell me more about human females. It seems I have much to learn."

"You know who would love this conversation?" she asks,

smiling as she bites into her second helping of fish. She seems relaxed now, the firelight dancing over her golden skin, her hair as bright as dawn in the sky. I like her like this.

I like her very much.

"Our crew's tech, Bex, is probably thrilled to be married to an alien. She is probably having the time of her life right now explaining female anatomy to her scaley husband."

Disappointment wrecks me, and the succulent taste of the fish turns to ash in my mouth. "I am sorry that this was not what you wanted, my prickly flower. I am sorry that I am not who you would choose, even though I would choose you one million times over. And not just because you are beautiful, not just because I would pick your face out of all the others in the galaxy, but because you are strong, stubborn, and resilient. You look delicate and fragile, and you are because you are human, but underneath that? You have as much mettle as any Suevan warlord on the battlefield."

It's more than I meant to say, but the Suevan language is meant for truths, and I will speak mine.

She stares at me for a moment, her eyes wide. "You know," she says conversationally, between bites, "we have a flower on my planet that's on a very thorny plant. It's called a cactus."

"It sounds formidable."

She shrugs, and there's a charming awkwardness to the gesture.

I realize something important about this human female.

She doesn't like the compliments. She doesn't like to be thought of as a flower or as fragile or as anything but a *survivor*—a fighter—which she is.

I grin at the realization. Because now? Now that I can understand her, now that I see a little more of who she is under that guarded wall... I can truly begin to woo her.

A sly smile spreads across her face, and she stretches languidly, her back against the wall, fire still flickering above her head.

"So, you wanted to know about human females, is that right?" Her voice is slightly husky, whether with exhaustion or something else, I do not know.

My attention hones in on her. "There is nothing I would rather know about, at the moment. About one in particular."

She laughs quietly, arching one eyebrow. "Then I'm going to tell you all about how to please one." There's a challenge in the statement, and I flex my muscles, meeting her stare.

"I very much like that idea." I am aroused and curious and my desire for this woman burns through me.

CHAPTER
NINE

GEN

KANUZ GAZE IS avid on mine, focused on me in a predatory way no human man has ever looked at me. It *devours* me, sending a tingling awareness through my body.

I clear my throat.

Maybe this isn't the best idea, discussing human anatomy with this alien. Maybe teasing him like this is ill-advised. He's not human, after all.

With him staring at me like that, the light-hearted and flirty *lesson* I had in my mind suddenly takes on a whole new dimension.

"Well, my cactus flower, are you going to speak on this pleasure, or are you going to simply stare at me and make me guess?" The question comes out on a growl, and a little shiver shakes me.

What would Bex say? Bex, no doubt, would be bold and sassy and hilarious, as she always is, and would probably leave the alien staring after her in awe and fear.

"We can orgasm many, many times in a row. Not all of us, of course, because everybody is different. But it's not too unusual for human females to come more than once with a skilled partner." I shrug, trying to appear unaffected.

I'm not.

Heat spreads across my chest, and I squirm a little against the ground, pressing my palms into my knees.

"Is this true?" he asks, delight and desire dancing across his face. "More than once a mating season?"

"Wait," I say, momentarily dumbfounded. "Did you say once a season? Suevan women can't come more than once a season? I must not be hearing you right." I shake my head.

"Only when they are breedable." He continues to stare at me as though I've grown three heads.

I gape at him. "That's awful."

"That is Suevan biology." There's a note of finality in his voice, and I realize too late I've insulted him somehow.

"Sorry," I say, rubbing my hands over my thighs. Next to me, my Federation issue tank dries slowly, and I feel exposed. "I am sorry for what's happened to the Suevan women. I didn't mean to offend you." The apology comes out easily.

Because it's true. It's not the sort of mealy-mouthed crap people say to one another when there's nothing else that comes to mind to fill the silence.

"I know what it's like to lose people you love," I say, unexpectedly emotional, my chest tightening. "I can't imagine what it would be like to think you're on the brink of extinction." I hate feeling like this, all emotional. I clear my throat again, and he regards me carefully.

"Thank you," he finally says. "Now—" His handsome smile reappears. "—I think you were telling me about human anatomy before we got off track." He edges closer, so close our knees touch.

My breath catches at the contact, and I know at once I've bitten off more I can chew by teasing this massive Suevan. My body goes tight and loose all at once at the thought of him acting on the promises he's made me, the blunt way he talks about being between my legs.

What the hell had I been thinking?

"Are you losing your nerve, little human?" he purrs, his eyes alight with humor. He licks the edge of one fang, and I toss my hair back, leaning my palms behind me.

"No, of course I'm not. I'm just figuring out how to describe it." Inhaling deeply, I scrunch my nose up and close my eyes. The sharp gravel chafes against the soft skin of my palm, and I focus on it, on the gentle lapping of the water against the walls of the pit.

"You seem tense," Kanuz whispers.

My eyes fly open at the warmth of his breath across my face. He's moved closer, his huge, muscled shoulders dwarfing me where I sit.

"I know what could relax you," he adds, but instead of smiling, his face is totally serious. "And though my species has suffered from the virus, I have had plenty of experience pleasing others. Tell me what to do."

His voice rings with command, and for once, for fucking once, I'm thankful for my stubborn, contrarian nature. Because it's a hell of a lot easier to say no when he uses that tone.

"I'll tell you what to do," I say, smirking up at him. My arms cross over my chest, and I'm all too aware of the fact my tank is still drying out on the rocks beside me.

His gaze flits to where my cleavage presses together under my sports bra, his tail flicking back and forth.

"But you're not going to touch me unless I tell you to. And it's not going to be tonight."

"Then I will have plenty of time to imagine how I will tear moans of pleasure from you, my prickly flower."

"Right." I try to keep my face blank and expressionless, but inside? Inside, I'm anything but blank. Who would have thought a huge, scaled alien dirty talking to me would be like my own personal catnip?

Bex, probably. A wave of sadness washes over me.

"What is wrong, Gen?" Kanuz' brow wrinkles slightly as he

lifts his brows, tenderness plain on his brutal face. "I did not mean to make you uncomfortable, my flower. I truly did not."

"No." I shake my head. "It's not that." It's sweet though, truly sweet, that he thinks he's made me uncomfortable even though I'm the one who started to play with fire only to immediately get burned. Affection wells in me, and I smile up at his unblinking face.

"Then why are you sad, Gen? Tell me. You have our words now. If you will not let me bring you to orgasm, then let me bring you solace. It is the very least I can do for my chosen female, for my princess."

A hoarse laugh rips out of my throat at the reminder that I am, in fact, a princess, and then I sniffle a little.

"Tell me, my flower," the Suevan prince says, then curls his big arm around me, pulling me into his lap in one fluid motion.

I'm tense at first, all that scaly green muscle caging me in, but he's warm, so warm, and his touch isn't searching or gross—it's comforting.

It catches me off guard, and I do as he says and speak my worries. "Do you think the rest of my crew is safe?"

"I will not lie to you, Gen," he says gravely, and my heart sinks. "I do not know if they are well or not, and I would not give you false hope. But what I will tell you is that each of your crew will be treasured by their mates, who are among the fiercest warlords Sueva has ever produced. If I had to guess, I would think that most are already safely ensconced in the myzas of Edrobaz. You are unlucky, to have been chosen by me, when another warlord may have been able to get you to safety sooner. As a prince, I did not receive the same training they did." His smile lacks humor, and his fingertips run over the bare skin of my arm. Carefully, he tucks my feet under his arm, frowning.

"You are cold."

"I'm okay. Food and fire for the win."

"I won something?" he asks, confusion curling his lip. The expression is so human, so at odds with the alien planet and the thick armored scales I'm resting against, that I can't help but laugh a little.

"It doesn't mean that, but you know what?" I sit up suddenly, and his hands slide against my stomach as I twist in his lap, kneeling against his thick thighs and taking his face in my hands. "How about this as a prize?"

I hesitate for a split second, knowing this is a bridge I can't uncross.

But right now, with his obscenely muscled chest pressed against mine, he's too tempting a distraction.

Why not?

His gaze captures mine, curious and as warm as the rest of him. The chill seeps from me the longer I spend with my skin against his, and for a moment, it's enough. It's enough to be held, to feel the thrum of his heart against my chest, to hold his warrior prince face in my hands.

And for some reason, it makes me heady with power, with the knowledge that he has had every opportunity to prove himself less than noble. But he isn't, and he's waiting for me to decide how far and fast I want to move.

So I brush my lips against his, my eyelashes fluttering shut. His hands tighten on my waist, then slip to my hips. His talons stroke gently across my skin, and I lose myself in the simple sensation of his touch. Of the feel of his full mouth against mine.

And suddenly, it's not enough.

I tease my tongue against the seam of his lips, and he opens his mouth with a groan. Desire rushes through me at the simple power of it, the tension radiating from him so at odds with the gentle pressure of his hands on my body. He's keeping himself leashed.

I'm not sure I want to see what happens when that carefully honed restraint finally cracks.

I pull away, and he sucks in a breath as I study the firelight flickering over the planes of his face.

"What was that for, my prickly flower?" he says.

Satisfaction rolls through me as I note how hoarse his voice is, further proof of how the chaste kiss affected him prodding against my ass as well.

"Because I felt like it," I say, and then confusion hits me again. This isn't some one-night stand with a Federation base boy-toy, this isn't even one of the semi-serious relationships I had before the Roth attack. I shouldn't play with the alien prince, not like this.

Any fun diversions we might get up to here, in this ruin, mean something much more than I wish they did.

I like the big alien prince, and as much as he's annoyed me, he's also saved my ass more than once.

But am I ready to be his wife? To have his babies?

I squirm, dislodging myself from his lap.

Or, at least, I attempt to, before he tugs me back.

"Ah-ah, my little human female. You are not going anywhere."

This time, he kisses me, and I melt against him, despite my reservations. His thick, rough tongue rasps against mine as he deepens the kiss, sending shivers of pleasure down my spine.

I turn away after a few seconds, feeling disheveled and frustrated and so confused about what I want.

"Now you will sleep, my wife, while I hold you and keep you warm. Because tomorrow will bring us many new challenges..." He runs a talon down the column of my throat, and there's a vicious victoriousness in his eyes that makes my blood sing. "...and you will need your strength for all of them."

I yawn then, the urge taking me by surprise. But what surprises me even more is how easy it is to relax against Kanuz, to let the lapping of the water on the walls and his steady breathing lull me to sleep.

And when he hums a low, haunting melody, my eyes drift shut, and I let sleep carry me away as the alien prince runs steady, gentle fingers through my hair.

CHAPTER
TEN

KANUZ

I DO NOT WISH to fall asleep. I could stare at this small golden female for hours on end. The way her lips part slightly in sleep, the gentle rise and fall of her chest, the way her eyes move under her eyelids.

What does she dream of, I wonder?

I brush the tips of my fingers across my lips, marveling at her trust, still shocked that she put her mouth on mine. That she wanted me enough to act on her instinct.

She is fierce and prickly as the cactus flower she told me about, but every inch of her is soft and so fragile.

My eyes close, and my grip tightens on the small human warrior.

Perhaps my father was right about me. Perhaps I am impulsive and lack what it takes to truly rule Sueva as it should be ruled.

Because now, with my heart's desire in my arms, I still want to find the many-faced goddesses' treasure.

What kind of husband does that make me, to risk the well-being of my chosen mate?

But what kind of husband would it make me to not take a chance to create a better future for her, for all of Sueva, if we can find the symbol of the goddesses' blessing and unite our people?

I cannot risk losing her; I cannot risk tearing my people apart any more than they already are.

A heavy sensation tightens my chest, and I watch Gen's breathing even out more as she falls more deeply asleep.

I will do everything in my power to keep her safe.

And right now, that means finding the treasure and ensuring we can have the future I so desperately want, the future Sueva so desperately needs. I can prove to my ailing father that I am fit to rule. I can prove to my Gen that I will be a good husband, the best mate. *And I will prove it to myself.*

The treasure is the key.

It's the only real chance at a future for any of us.

———

The fire still flickers when I wake, casting the same warm light. I blink a few times, confused about where I am, and it takes a moment for me to remember. In the ruined temple. The glossy wall and the pool both reflect the living flame in the wall, and it dances across Gen's sumptuous fall of hair.

She's so beautiful, so unlike any female I've ever seen, that I nearly stop breathing as I drink her in. My golden flower will be safe. I may not have been raised a warlord, but I am a prince, and I am confident in my ability to see us through the trials that the goddess and the ancients will have in store.

Her eyelashes flutter, and her eyes open wide, that crystalline blue piercing right through my heart as she gives me a long, sleepy look.

"Hi," she finally says, stretching long and languid. My eyes follow the curve of her breasts, the taut muscles of her abs, before tracking the plump curve of her ass and muscled thighs. I ache with the need for release.

"How did you sleep?" I ask.

She yawns, covering her mouth with a delicate hand, every-thing about her so fragile in the dull morning light. "I slept fine. How did you? Did you… Did you hold me all night?" She scoots away from me, her eyes wide with mortification. "That could not have been comfortable. You didn't have to do that."

"Of course, I had to hold you all night. I could not have my wife, a princess of Sueva, sleep on the cold stone floor." I shake my head, then tilt it, working out some of the knots that have, indeed, formed during the night. "It was my honor to hold you. It will always be my honor to hold you."

She blinks at that, her mouth round with surprise. "Ah, okay. Well, thank you. For, uh, holding me. All night." Her hands rub against her bare arms and she casts her gaze around until it lands on her shirt, dry on the rocks next to me.

I pick up the flimsy material and hold it out to her.

"You know, when we get back to Perzivor, I will have the finest garments made for you. Blue, I think, to match your pretty eyes."

"That's really not necessary," she says, plucking the shirt out of my hands and tugging it over her head. She pulls her hair out of the neck hole.

I snort, incredulous. "You would wear that every day? If you insist, I can have our tailors make you more pants and shirts, I suppose. But I would like to see you in the clothes of our people."

She pauses, tugging on the hem of her shirt, picking at a loose thread there, before narrowing her eyes at me.

I grin. I have grown to like that expression, like the challenge in it, and I ready myself for the barbed words I'm sure are on the tip of her tongue.

"I'm not a doll or a pet to be dressed up. I'm a First Officer of the Federation, and I'm here to…" She clears her throat. "I was here to make sure that Earth got the tech we need to protect ourselves from further Roth invasions, as you know."

"You are here as my wife." I stand up slowly, stalking toward her. She holds her ground, and my smile deepens further. "The tech is on the way to Earth. And what you wear has nothing to do with who you are to the Federation. You are also a Princess of Sueva now." I tilt my head, studying her. "If you do not want to wear our garments, that is your choice. You are stunning no matter what you wear. Or what you don't wear." I flash some fang at her, and her throat bobs.

"I just…" She rakes her hand through her golden locks, and her fingers snag on the tangled ends. I frown. I should have combed it for her. I haven't cared for another in a long time. Sure, I have been with my choice of females, but that was different.

I *want* to care for this prickly human.

I want her to look to me and see safety, see comfort.

To see her future. Our future.

And for that future to be safe, we have to keep moving. We have to solve the riddle of this place, and get to Edrobaz, then move on to Perzivor, where our home and future await.

And in the meantime, she will fall in love with me, and accept her place by my side.

I remember the way her lips felt on mine last night, and I take another step closer.

"Do you want to kiss me again, wife? Would that convince you that you might like being mine? I can think of other places to kiss, if you need even more convincing."

She makes a strangled noise, pinching the bridge of her nose.

ELEVEN

GEN

WHY DOES he keep offering to eat me out?

The better question is, why in the *world* am I considering say yes?

I'm in a freaking pit, in a ruined temple, on an alien planet with angry dinosaurs outside, and part of me is like, *sure, yeah, let's get down and dirty with the alien prince who keeps offering oral like it's a party favor at the universe's worst party* ever.

All I can do is stare at him.

The queen of comebacks is all out of witty repartee.

He laughs quietly, like he knows I'm thinking about it, goddammit, and he probably does know it, considering he can oh, I don't know, *scent my arousal*?!

I would like to do a big scream, but I'm too afraid something gnarly and alien is going to pop out of the water behind me and chomp me like a mid-morning snack.

"No, thank you," I say stiffly. *Look at you, Genevieve Durand, making good choices, and so polite, too!*

"Do humans not like that?" His tail lashes behind him.

I rub my face.

"You never did tell me about human mating rituals."

"It's too early for this conversation. I need coffee. Food."

"I do not know this kaw-fee." He shakes his head, forlorn, and it's adorable.

I mentally smack myself. No. He is not adorable. I cannot think about him like that! I can't catch feelings for this alien. I can kiss him, I can appreciate his ability to keep me safe, I can appreciate his ridiculously hot body, but I cannot catch feelings.

No. I cannot stay here. I cannot be a princess. I'm at least ninety-nine percent sure. I am one hundred percent sure that these are also problems for future Gen. Current Gen just needs to get the fuck to safety. I keep rubbing my face, trying to sort myself out.

"Are you all right, my flower? You are going to hurt your eyeballs if you continue to rip at them with your tiny claws."

My hands fall away from my face, and I stare up at him. "Tiny claws?"

"Perhaps I was wrong," he shrugs. "They do not look fearsome, after all."

I frown, staring at my fingernails. I never thought I would feel insulted by someone saying my nails weren't capable of savaging eyeballs, but here I am. Just chock-full of new experiences!

"I will catch you something to eat, my cactus flower. Then we will set off on our great adventure."

"Ah—" Before I can finish whatever I was about to say, Kanuz strips his pants back off, diving into the pool.

Sudden fear trickles over me. What if something happens to him in there? What if there is an alien monster in there, and it chomps him for second breakfasts?

"Potatoes," I moan, backing up from the pool. Why didn't I disobey orders and bring a damn weapon to that stupid ass ceremony? The ceremony where I wound up married?!

Well, at least I know now why the Federation was so fucking weird about us participating in their ceremony fully.

My hands fist at my sides, a fresh wave of hot anger washing over me. Those slimy motherfuckers.

Kanuz pops up a second later, a whitish-translucent fish in either hand. "Look, my flower! We will have enough to bring some along."

"Yay," I manage. "Any chance of po-tay-toes down there, too?" I laugh at my own joke, but it's a high, strained sound.

"I do not have kaw-fee, and I do not have po-tay-toes." Kanuz sighs, shaking his head as he tosses the still-flopping fish near the fiery wall. "I only have the fish, my Gen."

"It's all good." I nearly correct him on calling me *his* Gen, but I don't. Why bother? It has nothing to do with the little warm fuzzies I have now.

Probably.

He beams at me, his tail swishing behind his powerfully sculpted butt, his thick thighs corded with muscle. I don't even look at his dick. Much.

"Any chance you know where to start getting us out of here this morning?" I ask, watching as he easily cleans the fish with nothing but his scary ass talons. Geez. No wonder he was worried about me scratching my eyes out. Now I'm worried about him scratching my—

"You always have those talons?" I cringe at my own random question.

He looks up slowly from the gutted fish, that same self-satisfied smile tugging up the corners of the fish. "Why are you thinking about my talons?"

"Just curious."

"I can rid myself of them, if you are worried, my flower." He purrs.

I turn away, staring at the etchings in the glossy wall. "Anyway!" I nearly yell it, managing to startle myself as the sound echoes off the solid wall. "Where do we go after we eat? I don't see a door, or a handle, or anything." Now that I'm awake enough to think about it, my lips twist to the side.

God, I hope there wasn't a damn door here all night. I slept really great, amazingly well, in Kanuz's arms, but the thought of there being a door here, leading to who knows what… It freaks me out.

Why *did* I sleep so well last night? Exhaustion and a full stomach for once. Yeah. That's gotta be it.

"There is no door. Not right now," he says cheerfully. He's standing right beside me, and I startle again.

The fish sizzles where he holds it against the flames still burning on the wall. It smells amazing, and my mouth waters.

"There is a riddle at the end of this wall. We have to solve it before the goddess will allow us to move on." He hands me a skewer of fish.

"Thanks," I tell him. Potatoes and second breakfasts aside, I'm beyond grateful for more food. "Before the goddess allows us? What does that mean?"

His tail thumps against the floor, and my gaze darts to it. Gah! He's still pantsless. "It means that we have to solve the riddle before we can leave this chamber."

Sure, why not? "Think we can be out of here today?"

"Perhaps," he says slowly, heating his own skewer of fish. "Perhaps the goddess will smile down on us and decide we are worthy sooner than later."

"So not likely, then." I blow out a breath, making a frustrated raspberry sound.

He shakes his head, amusement sparking in his eyes. "My flower, I enjoy your company very much. You are like sunshine given life."

I snort. "Yeah, right." No one's ever said I had a sunny disposition before, and I laugh some more, before quieting. Well, no one's said it since the Roth attacked. Maybe I used to be.

I finish off the rest of the fish in silence. Kanuz doesn't speak either, though it's not an awkward quiet. No, it's companionable, like the quiet a married couple who's been together a very long time might have after breakfast.

Good grief. I am *married*. It doesn't seem quite real, probably because we married in their Suevan tradition and I had no idea it was happening, but still! There's the proof, all near seven scaled feet of him, grinning at me when he catches my eye.

Now that I can talk to him, really talk to him, that is, not play that terrible version of survivor charades, it's easier to be in a good mood.

I guess communication is the key to a good marriage, after all.

I snort at myself, washing my hands off in the pool, before cupping them and drinking deeply.

"Take off your shirt," Kanuz tells me, kneeling beside me and cleaning his own hands, using some of the gritty gravel to scrub his talons.

"What?"

"We can use your shirt to carry the cooked fish in. I will knot it into a little pouch for you."

I sigh. I can't fault the logic of it. It makes sense, considering the delicate flesh of the fish would get smashed to smithereens in the crappy pockets of my uniform pants.

"Fine." I tug it overhead, and Kanuz makes quick work of it, depositing the chunks of cooked fish into the fabric before handing it back to me. "Do I just hold it?" It feels weird to hold my own shirt, full of fish, and for a second, I don't know what to do with my hands.

"You are like a youngling." He laughs. "Here." Kanuz takes the makeshift pouch from me. "I will fasten it to you."

His talons scrape gently across the waistband of my pants, and I shudder at his unexpected touch. Not a bad shudder, either, but an excited shake that sends goosebumps all over my skin.

"Why are you bumpy?"

"It's just a thing human skin does sometimes. I have no idea." I frown, his dick all too close for comfort. "Why are *you* bumpy?" He is, too, his rock-hard alien eggplant covered in texture. "That's not, like, diseased, is it?"

"Diseased?!" His tone is offended, and I snort again, glancing up at him. "I am not diseased."

"I don't know! You keep bragging about how many women you've slept with."

"Diseased," he mutters to himself. "Diseased, me, the prince of Sueva. You humans have strange ideas."

I resist the urge to poke his cock out of sheer curiosity, clenching my hands into fists. He's too close. Too warm. Too muscled. I squeeze my eyes shut, because truly, that's the only way I'm getting his bumpy dick out of my line of sight. Sure, I cuddled up with the jolly green giant last night, but this feels… different. Like my whole body is awake and aware of him.

"It is not a disease, my flower. Those are my pleasure bumps. If you were not holding your blue eyes closed, you would see how they are bigger for you the harder I get. They will make you feel good, so good, as I thrust inside you, filling you with my pleasure." His voice is a husky whisper.

I bite my cheeks. It should be funny, right? This alien prince telling me about how he's going to fuck me silly with his sex toy cock, bumped for my pleasure… but it is not. It is not funny, because my stupid body is clenching in anticipation.

Why does dirty talk have to be my thing and why does Kanuz have to keep TALKING DIRTY?!

"Riddle!" I yell out. "Let's solve the riddle and put pants on! Pants and riddles! They go together like potatoes and coffee!"

"Why are you shouting at me, Gen? Is your translator failing again?" Worry creases his forehead. "Those damn symbionts. I told my scientists that they could be too untrustworthy. They have a mind of their own, you know."

"Symbiont?" I tug at my earlobe. "I can't. You know what? I really can't with that. That's one too many facts for me right now."

"It is a perfectly safe creature, Gen, I promise you that, they are just a little temperamental. Which is why I told my scientists to look for another—"

"I really don't want to hear anymore. I really don't want to hear about it." I shake my head again, trying to dislodge that extremely disgusting new information. Alas, my brain is not an etch-a-sketch.

"Do humans often argue and yell when they are aroused? You are a confusing female."

"No. Yes." I throw my hands in the air, narrowly missing slapping the still-too-close Kanuz. "Focus," I yell again, mainly talking to myself. "Let's get going so we can get out of here."

"I, too, am eager to begin making our family together, my flower," he says agreeably. Ugh. He's so cute when he smiles at me like that, like I'm his whole world.

A woman could get used to that kind of thing. "That's not... I want to see my crew," I say faintly.

"Because you are a good leader." He nods. "You must see to them before you can focus on swelling with our young."

Ew. "That isn't the most ideal description."

"I long to see you heavy with my child, Gen, so that everyone knows the future of Sueva is secure, and so that everyone knows that you are mine. For our scents to mix all over your irresistible body..." He sighs, and I swear to god, his dick jerks.

"Then we better get started on this damn temple," I tell him, caught somewhere between annoyance and unwilling affection.

It's just so *cute*, how he wants a family. I have an IUD, so there's no way I'm swelling with anyone's young, least of all my accidental alien husband, but it's cute all the same. He'd probably be a great dad. He's funny and patient, and he's taken good care of me, for all we were irritated at not being able to communicate for too long.

I cut off that line of thinking.

"Yes, the dam temple," he says. "Let us begin." He rubs his hands together, one eyebrow raising mischievously.

I laugh in spite of myself. "Pants."

"Pants," he agrees, pulling them on.

I should look away, really, I should. But it's more fun to watch his muscles do muscly things as he tugs the tight fabric into place.

When he catches me watching, his smile is dazzling, and my heart skips a beat.

If I'm being honest with myself, he's hot for an alien. He's hot for a human.

I'm hot for the alien prince.

"If you look at me like that, I will not be able to focus, as you keep asking me to do."

"I'm not looking." *Busted.*

"You are looking, my sweet flower, and I am glad for it."

"Temple," I shout, as though I'm declaring sanctuary.

"Temple," he agrees, turning to face the wall. His back is so thickly slabbed with muscle it's a wonder he isn't the illustration in anatomical studies. I tilt my head, taking in his massive tail. For all I know, he might be, here on Sueva.

"The riddle is here," he says, walking to where the glossy wall butts up against the rough hewn stone the rest of the pit's made from.

I follow him, the Federation tank/fish pouch swaying against my hip as I move.

His talon traces along the edges of a snake carved into the wall, the eye of it a glittering prism standing out even against the highly polished surface. The head and the eye rest in the center of the coils, where they fan out in an ever-wider pattern.

I frown. There's something familiar about it, but I can't quite put my finger on it.

"Here and here," Kanuz murmurs, his voice low as he puzzles over it. He points to a sequence of characters next to it that make absolutely no sense to me.

"What do those say?"

"They're numbers. There's no rhyme or reason to them." He shrugs one shoulder, and I lick my lips. "There is no sequence, no pattern that I can determine. And I was taught by the best scholars and mathematicians on the planet." His frown deepens. "Just a random jumble."

He moves his finger around, and I gape.

The numbers—the alien characters—move.

"The fuck?" I ask. "Is it a touchscreen? I feel like an idiot sandwich." This whole time, I thought it was just shiny ass rock.

But no. The ancients of Sueva apparently figured out how to build a perma-touch screen that functions after years of disuse.

Ridiculous.

"Of course, it is. How else would we be able to solve the riddle?" Kanuz turns to me, clearly bewildered. "What is an idiot meal?"

"That's a great question." I'm not going to tell him I half imagined we were in a Wizard of Oz scenario, where some actual deity was hanging out behind a curtain, waiting to bless our shiny red slippers. Or combat boots, whichever. "This is cool." I run the pads of my fingertips over the numbers, and they wave and flicker under my touch, moving when I reorganize them. I don't have a clue what they mean, but it's still fun.

"And, ah, it's idiot sandwich. It's just a silly saying. I don't think I can explain it." I shrug one shoulder.

"I would make a meal of you, but it would not be a stupid one." His tail lashes back and forth. "I would—"

"So we have a snake, and a bunch of numbers," I interrupt. "Is there some kind of myth with a snake and numbers in your religion?"

"Not that I recall. Perhaps..." He purses his lips, his fingers darting over the surface. "Perhaps if I use the numbers that correspond to the letter order and drop them in the snake..." he stops talking, dumping a sequence of numbers into the interior of the snake.

I stare at the characters in the coils, willing something to happen.

Nothing does. Instead, they flicker, then disappear before reappearing in the number pile again.

Numbers inside the snake. It triggers a memory in me, but when I grasp at it, the idea eludes me. I fucking hate when that shit happens. Why is it always when you need to remember something the most your brain just gives you the middle finger and goes back to sleep?

"Serpent?" I ask hopefully.

He shrugs. "Worth a try." The numbers are added to the coils again. Nothing.

"Perhaps the name of the many-faced goddess' snake avatar." He tries a new combination, and I suck in a breath once I realize I've been holding mine.

The numbers disappear again.

"Maybe we should have started this last night."

"I enjoyed what we did last night."

"We slept," I say, a low laugh coming out of me. "It was nice to be out of the rain for once, though."

"I held my mate all night," Kanuz growls, and this time, irritation and hurt flicker over his aggressively masculine features. "There is nothing in this temple that could top that."

"Oh." I blink. "That was nice, too."

"Nice," he rasps, turning back to the wall—touchscreen—and jabbing at it ferociously.

My nose wrinkles. Isn't it too soon for him to get his feelings hurt in this… relationship? Marriage? I mean, we only just started communicating. Sure, I kissed him last night, but this is a whole new level of stage five clinger.

The weirdest part is… it's kinda cute. Why do I think it's so *cute*?!

I watch him poke at the wall, staring at the coiled snake and letting my mind drift over our weeks together.

And then it hits me.

"Fuck yeah," I say, a bit breathless as the thought bowls through me. "Fibonacci." The word bursts out of me, and I tilt my head, considering. "That's it. It's a Fibonacci spiral. The Fibonacci sequence."

"The what?" Kanuz is watching me, his eyes narrowed, diamond-pupils fixed on my face.

"Oh." I blow out a breath, deflated. "Yeah, I guess you wouldn't call it that, huh? Uh, lemme try to explain." Math wasn't my strong suit. Am I terrible at it? No. Is it my favorite? Also no. "Uh, okay, so there was this dude named Fibonacci, and he figured out this sequence of numbers, where they, like... fit together. Each one is the sum of the previous two numbers, and if you..." I trail off, closing one eye, like that's going to help me concentrate. "If you create a physical representation, it makes a perfect spiral."

"The sunshine ratio," he says, his eyes wide, an expression of awe on his face. "Of course, you would know that, my golden flower."

Okay, so we've progressed to a *golden flower*. Still, I can't help a little shiver of pleasure and pride at the starstruck look in his eyes. No one has ever looked at me like that, like life's a puzzle and I hold all the answers.

Call me Fibonacci, I guess.

"I will try it," he declares, his fingers whirring over the screen as he dumps characters into the spiral of the snake.

The numbers dissolve into nothing, and I exhale noisily. Damn. I was so sure I'd cracked it. Kanuz places a heavy hand on my shoulder.

"It was an excellent idea," he says.

The snake collapses in on itself, the jewel of the eye falling out of the screen. Kanuz's hand whips out, and he catches it before it can hit the stone and gravel ground.

"Holy shit, I did it! I feel like fucking Indiana Jones!" I'm screeching, way too excited about going deeper into this death trap of a temple.

When Kanuz straightens, his expression is dark, iciness replacing the warmth that breathed in his gaze only moments ago.

A seam appears in the wall, and an arched door swings open where the snake and numbers once hung out. Kanuz nods at me.

"Well done," he says, but it's cold. I stare up at him, utterly confused at his sudden tone change. Talk about whiplash.

"Thanks?"

His face softens briefly, but then he frowns. The interior of the newly opened chamber is dark, and I press myself closer to him.

"I can't see in there," I whisper. I'm not really sure why I'm whispering, but the need to keep quiet steals over me.

"Maybe you should ask your Indiana Jones for help," he says stiffly.

My nose scrunches up, and I tilt my head in confusion, trying to get a read on him.

"What?"

"The Indiana Jones you want to fuck," he says.

Realization dawns on me, and I choke back a laugh. It's not funny, not really. I bite my cheeks. His feelings are hurt because I said I felt like *fucking* Indiana Jones. I have to clamp my mouth shut to keep the laugh inside.

"That's not," I finally gasp out, "that's not what I meant. Indiana Jones isn't real. It's a character. From a story. A movie."

His brow furrows. "You want to fuck a figment of your imagination?"

I can't help it. A huge laugh barks out of me, and then I'm gasping for air. If Bex were here, she'd be having a field day with this. She would likewise be fucking the hot alien, that's for damn sure. I hope my girl is getting hers.

The thought brings me up short, and I blow out a shaky, near-hysteric breath.

"No. Okay, let me back up." I inhale slowly, forcing myself to calm down. "Indiana Jones is a cool explorer dude, a total badass, although the colonial appropriation is pretty problematic. But regardless! He was an archaeologist, and he went on all these dangerous adventures. I meant that I *felt* like him. Cool, and smart, and hot, and all that good stuff. The fucking was just… an adjective."

My lips twist to the side, because I'm not sure how well I've conveyed my thought process or whether or not fucking is an adjective at all, and trying to explain my random statement makes me sound fairly unhinged.

"You feel cool and hot at the same time?" Worry tinges his voice now.

Exasperated, I slam a hand against my forehead. "No. It's figurative. Cool is good. Hot is like… sexy."

"You are scorching hot, my flower. An inferno."

"Right."

"So you do not want to fuck this imaginary explorer?"

My eyebrows go up. He's jealous. He's envious of Indiana Jones, which somehow makes him seem more human than ever.

"I cannot stand the thought of you with another male, my golden flower." He doesn't wait for me to answer, which is probably a good thing, considering the question and my propensity for blunt honesty. He tugs me closer to him, his huge hand bracketing my shoulder.

Together, we trudge through the archway and deeper into the temple of gloom and doom.

The door slams shut behind us, and a grinding reverberates through the room, rattling my teeth.

I sway as the ground rumbles, and Kanuz sweeps me up into his arms a second later, snarling at nothing I can see.

"What is it?" I whisper. I wish I had my gun.

Light cascades through the chamber, the line of fire igniting in thick whorls and swirls along the stone walls, and I see what it is that has Kanuz's hackles raised. Literal and figurative hackles.

The walls are covered in spikes. A white ribcage hangs from one, a skull on another.

And they're pressing closer.

Towards where Kanuz holds me tight against him.

How the hell are we going to get out of this?

KANUZ

I AM AN IDIOT. I never should have brought my mate into this temple. What was I thinking?

My father would be so disappointed. Worse, he would be unsurprised.

I grind my teeth together.

"What do we do, Kanuz? Where is the riddle?" My Gen's voice is even and serious, none of her usual mirth and sarcasm present.

She is counting on me.

I snap out of my self-loathing.

"There," I tell her, jerking my head towards the far wall. I glance back, just in case, but sure enough, the arched door has disappeared again. The only way out is forward.

"I don't see it," she says. "Put me down and let's run for the other side. From the looks of it, we don't have a lot of time. That guy is for sure out of time." She nods at the skull hanging on the opposite wall.

I do not do as she asks. Instead, I carry her to where the newest puzzle lies.

"I am glad you are my partner in this," I tell her. "You solved the last where I would not have."

"Nah, you would've gotten it together eventually."

It's not exactly a rousing endorsement of my intelligence, but I smile at her nonetheless, sprinting to the far wall.

"This is a word puzzle. Child's play."

"If you can read the language, I suppose. For me, it would be xenolinguistic's play. Or doctoral dissertation, more likely. And my crew member who'd kill at this, Michelle, isn't here." She chuckles, but the sound lacks her normal humor.

She is frightened. It is my fault for bringing her here. For thinking we could easily obtain the goddess' blessing and find our way through this temple.

"It is all right, little female," I tell her, setting her down. Her worried gaze flits between the ancient script on the wall and me. Around us, the sound of stone-on-stone grates ceaselessly, the spikes coming closer with every minute.

This is not just a language test. This is a test of nerves under pressure, something that my father always complained I did not have. That I was too selfish, too cocksure, too inexperienced to be able to manage any tasks to his liking.

But now I have my mate to think of, and I squelch the sound of my father's complaints in my head. There is no room for his disdain now. There is only my Gen, and our combined need to leave this place.

I interlace my fingers with hers, careful to keep the sharp points of my talons away from her delicate skin. There is something about her that grounds me. Her steady gaze on me, trusting, despite all I have already put her through, since the first moment we sealed our bond in the wedding ceremony. Despite her thorny nature and sometimes thorny words, my Gen looks to me with hope and a trusting calm that makes my heart hurt.

I cannot let her down.

I will not.

Her hand squeezes against mine, and I feel it all the way in my chest.

I take a deep breath, and I begin reordering the words. For once, I am thankful for the endless lessons spent with the priestesses of the many-faced-goddess, something younger me would no doubt be agog at.

Because I recognize these words. Even in my state of heightened anxiety, my fear for my sweet golden human next to me spiking the closer the sharp points get, I recall them easily.

"For it is not the blossom of spring or the chill of winter, nor the first zitsu leaf of fall or the flood of the rainy season. It is none of these things, and it is all of them. She is in the riotous crack of thunder, the smile of sunlight, and the glint of water in moonlight. The many-faced-goddess is everywhere, and she speaks the language of truth."

As soon as I slot the last word into place, the walls grind to a stop, the closest spike nudging against my hip.

"You did it. Oh my god, you did it," Gen whispers, and as she sucks in a shaky breath, it hits me again, how foolish I've been to endanger her like this.

A new door swings open ahead of us, and the next room is not dark at all.

I'm so focused on what's beyond, on my task of getting us out of here, that I don't realize she's wreathed her small hands around my neck until she gives my head a forceful tug.

And when her lips find mine again, possessive, searching, I nearly fucking lose my mind.

CHAPTER
THIRTEEN

GEN

I'M JUST SO glad I didn't get squished to death. I'm surfing the wave of adrenaline, hanging ten like a badass, and all I meant to do was hug Kanuz.

And then the next thing I know, I'm kissing the daylights out of him.

It feels really fucking great, too, like the whole damn death trap temple disappears from around us, leaving only the feeling of his hands on my back, his gentle mouth against mine.

It's not enough. I want more.

I open my mouth, and he groans, his textured tongue rasping against my teeth. A taloned hand slides into my hair, tugging my head back as the kiss deepens. It's not just a kiss anymore.

It's a *claiming*.

It sears across my body, and desire shoots through me as Kanuz proves that all his practice did, in fact, make perfect.

My alien prince is a *great* kisser.

My alien prince? I pull up short, some sense finally driving itself into my skull.

Better sense than a sharp spike, I guess.

My breath's coming in hard pants, like I've just run a mile. Kanuz stares down at me, his diamond pupils so dilated his eyes are nearly full black.

"Where do you think you are going?" he asks, the question husky and rough. His mouth slams into mine, his hand possessive and tight on the back of my neck. I *love* it.

I wriggle closer to him, giving in to the need to touch him, the need to feel the hard, reassuring muscle packed tight on him. He groans his approval, the sound blazing through me. *More. Faster.*

His tongue flicks against mine, rough and bumped and completely alien. I run my hands up the jacked curves of his biceps, and he tugs my head closer still, his other hand making gentle circles on the small of my back.

Shivers run down my spine, dampness pooling between my legs.

Something thick wraps around my ankle, and I break off the kiss in alarm only to realize it's his *tail*.

"Okay," I say, pulling away. "Good job." My voice is unsteady and breathy and not at all like me.

"Why do you run from me, Gen?" Kanuz grates out, his body taut.

I want to rub my hands all over him. His skin—hide?—is tough, but smoother than it looks, and all that muscle? *Yum*.

But I don't. I stare up at him, wild-eyed and breathless, and I don't know what to do with myself.

"Is this some human courtship game? To make me want you until I am mad with needing to feel you deep inside?"

Oh god, not the dirty talk again.

"I just, Kanuz, I know you think we're married—"

"We are married, *wife*."

"Okay, but here's the thing, I don't know if I can be what you want me to be." The statement spills out of me, and I blink, surprised by my own honesty.

Surprised by what I'm even freaking *saying*.

Because my rejection isn't because of him. It's not. The dang jolly green alien giant wormed his way into my brain. I *want* him.

He blinks slowly, his third eyelid retracting.

"Kanuz, I'm not a princess. I'm not a Suevan. This is all moving really fast. While I'd like to take a ride on the Prince Kanuz train, I know you're just going to be upset when we're back with the rest of your people." *If we get back.* "I'm not ready for kids. Younglings. Babies. Like, not at all. In fact, I have an IUD—"

"I do not know this word." He steps closer, his hands on my hips as he pulls me to him again. *Ooh, I like that.* Concern wrinkles his brow. "Are you ill? Did you leave a lover behind on Earth? Now that I know you did not come willingly…" Kanuz breaks off, staring at me with wide, open eyes.

"No, I have a—" I pause, casting around for the right word. "I have a thing inside me. It stops me from getting pregnant. It keeps your swimmers from meeting up with my eggs." Eggs. "Oh god, you don't expect me to lay an egg, do you?"

"I do not even know how to answer that question. Are you asking about how Suevan's reproduce? We do not lay eggs." He huffs a laugh, affection curling his lips into a small smile. "Our females gave birth, like yours. That is *why* we are a compatible species. Does that mean you are thinking about expelling this device? For me?" His fingers clench on my hips, and I nearly moan at the contact, at the clear desire in his touch.

"I can't *expel* it. And no." I shake my head. "No lover, not any that mattered. And no? I'm not thinking about expelling it?" But I say it like a question, and it's clear from the look on his face that he thinks he's persuaded me. I'm confused, because suddenly, I am imagining it. I am. And it freaks me right the fuck out. "Kanuz, seriously. I just… This timing is bad. Listen." I take a step back from the alien looking like Christmas came early.

I swallow hard. Now is not the time to think about anything *coming*, Christmas or not.

"Tell me, my golden flower," he murmurs, watching me carefully.

"I gave up all hope of a family after the Roth came to Earth. This is… This is a huge adjustment. I realize that the Federation is likely not going to accept us back with open arms." A pang goes through my chest. "But… I don't think I can just undo years worth of changing what I wanted after the Roth invasion."

His grin deepens, and he closes the distance between us with two powerful steps. "Then I see no problem at all."

"But you want babies. That's like… the whole point of me being here. Of all of us being here." I close my eyes, concern for the rest of the crew resurfacing. God, I bet they're spitting bullets. "Right?" I open my eyes.

His hand cups my face, and his smile's gone, replaced by an intent focus that has my toes curling in my boots.

"You do not want children."

"Not right now," I agree. I never in a million years thought I'd be having this conversation, let alone having it with my alien prince *husband*.

"You cannot have children, because of your device," he adds, his smile returning.

"Correct." I frown at him, confused at his delight.

"Then I see no problem with me thrusting deep inside you, my flower." His thumb strokes across my cheekbone.

It takes me a minute to process what he's said. "Wait—"

"I am tired of waiting," he growls, tilting my head back once more. I close my eyes, preparing for the feel of his mouth against mine.

When it doesn't come, I gaze up at him, confused.

"But I will wait as long as you need to be ready, Gen. In the meantime, let us proceed to the next *delightful* chamber the goddess has in store for us."

I can't help but smile at his obvious sarcasm, even though I'm still weak-kneed and wanting.

I suck in a deep breath, and Kanuz trails his hand down my

bare arm, only to close it around my hand, like he needs to be touching me at all times.

It's really sweet, and tiny butterflies take flight in my stomach. Who knew a massive, taloned, scary ass alien would be a bigger, sexier softie than any man I dated on Earth?

Not me!

The warm fuzzies don't last long, however. As soon as we walk through the door, it slams behind us, so hard it sends grit and dust cascading down in a thick cloud. Nothing like a shower of sharp rock to cut off any sexy ideas.

I throw my arm over my head on instinct. It's not necessary, though, seeing as how Kanuz tackles me, diving to the floor with me in his arms as though he expects the ceiling to cave in at any moment. He traps me under his big body, and I curl up around myself. Just in case he's not overreacting, and the ceiling *is* about to bury us alive.

A full body shudder shakes me.

It's one thing to face a platoon of angry Roth aliens with my weapons spitting hellfire, but it's another to think about the possibility of being buried alive.

My throat closes up, and a small whimper erupts from my throat.

"My flower, are you hurt?" Kanuz's gaze scans me from head to toe, his expression turning thunderous. "You are bleeding." I wince as he gently runs a fingertip across a gash in my forehead.

It doesn't hurt, though, which is either a sign I'm truly fucked… or that it's not *that* bad. I take a deep breath and force my breathing to slow before touching it myself. Gingerly, I explore the small cut and bump, before exhaling a huge sigh of relief.

"It's nothing," I tell him. "One of the rocks must have caught me before you threw yourself over me like a massive alien blanket."

"My hide is more well-equipped than your fragile skin." His voice is pitiful, and I blink up at him. "It is my fault you are injured. I should have found a way out of the jungle by now. We should be in Edrobaz, sipping their delicious cold drinks and pleasuring each other. Instead, you are bleeding and dirty."

"It's really not a big deal. I'm not concussed. Besides, we can't sit here and worry about what we should have done. You need to put on our big boy alien pants so we can get the hell out of here. We don't have time to look back. I'd like one of those drinks, when we get there."

"Big boy alien pants are the only pants I have." He stares down at me mournfully, and I wipe away the blood and grit smeared on my face.

I snort a laugh, and a small smile tugs up one corner of his mouth. Like this, with his oversized body pressed up against mine, I'm all too aware of him. It's more intimate than some kisses I've had back on Earth. My body goes hot all over, and something changes in Kanuz, too, like he's in tune with me.

Shit. He's probably doing his weird arousal sniff again.

But I mean, if I'm going to be buried alive, maybe death during a dicking down wouldn't be the worst way to go. I shake my head a little. Maybe I *am* concussed, because that's not a great idea.

"What are you thinking about?" he asks, his arms caging me in. My breathing quickens, and I nearly tell him.

"How a hot bath and some soap sound like heaven when we get out of here," I lie. "Nothing better than some pampering post-near-death experience."

Another cloud of dust explodes overhead, and he pushes me into his chest, cradling me.

"I would pamper you, my Gen. I would pamper every inch of your body, until you cannot even think of this anymore, until all you can think of is me."

I gotta be honest, it's sounding better and better the more he talks about it.

"You make a lot of promises, my dude." I try to keep my voice light, try not to let on how scared and worried I am. "You could really get a girl's hopes up high."

"I heard no complaints about my kiss," he says. His voice is strained, rock and grit continuing to shake free of the ceiling overhead.

"Mmm..." I say, shrugging against his chest, my small smile hidden against his skin.

"What is this *mmm*?" he asks, and this time, there's consternation in the question.

I bite my cheeks.

"What do you mean by *mmm*? What does this *mmm* mean?" He glances down at me, eyes narrowed. "You did not melt against me to make this mmm sound. You did not fill my nose with the scent of your cunt just to tell me it was *mmm*. You were wet for me," he accuses. "Do not pretend otherwise."

"Mmm," I hum agreeably, and he tilts his head, inspecting me as though I'm a greater mystery than this damn temple.

Finally, the temple finishes vibrating. I exhale. We're not going to be buried alive.

Yet.

A few more rocks tumble down, the last-minute drama queens. Kanuz eyes them warily before standing. The look he gives them promises death, which would be hard to do, even for the muscle-bound alien prince of Sueva, considering they're *rocks*.

"I will not hear this *mmm* from you," Kanuz says to where I sit on the ground, stretching my neck out.

"Mmm," I repeat, trying not to laugh.

"You are teasing me," he says. "You think to tease me about my prowess in mating?" There's no humor to the question, his tail slashing the air behind him. "I will show you, my little human flower, and then you will not make this *mmm* noise again."

A tiny shiver of anticipation goes through me, silencing the spark of humor. Kanuz continues to stare at me, rolling his shoulders. When he winces, I stand up, ignoring the pain jolting through me.

"You're hurt."

"Better me than you," he says. "And I am fine. Now, let us

discover the surprises this room holds. That is, if you can concentrate while you think about having sex with me."

"Excuse me," I exclaim, putting my hands on my hips. "The only one thinking about sex is *you*, Prince!"

His fangs flash as his smile deepens, his tail slapping the ground. "You are a pretty little liar."

"Argh!" I throw my hands up in frustration, taking stock of the latest room in this stupid labyrinth temple. I gotta get out of here. I'm stuck in this year's production of Alien Indiana Boner and the Temple of Gloom, because the alien who *married* me can't think past his magic stick.

The room's filled with rock dust, and I wave my hand in front of my face, trying to clear it. I reach for the tank knotted to my belt loop… and come up with a handful of smashed fish.

"Gross," I mutter.

"I am sorry," Kanuz says. "I did not imagine the ceiling would give in and crush our meal."

"Can't say I blame you on that one," I say, wrinkling my nose and tossing the fishy fabric far away.

There's water in this room too, a huge dark pool, and the sealed off entrance to the last trap. I squint, in the dim light cast by the line of fire embedded in the wall, trying to see if there's another touchscreen anywhere.

Nope. The walls are all rough stone, no carvings, no symbols, nothing.

Just the dark, rippling expanse of water stretching before us.

I purse my lips.

"I have a feeling we're going to have to go in there," I tell Kanuz.

He grunts in agreement, his movements stiff.

I can't say I love the idea of getting in it. The pool isn't nearly as inviting as the last one, and that one was about as inviting as a shark-infested riptide.

I mean, some people might be into that kind of thing, but I'm not.

Shit. I wish I hadn't thought of sharks.

"There isn't anything… living in here, right?" I peer at the pool. "Besides dinner? Or is it lunch?" I don't have a clue what time it is.

"There may be fish." He lingers on the last word, drawing it out in a way that tells me he's worried about whateverthefuck might be lurking in there, too.

I take a hasty step away from the pool.

Well, at least I can't be scared and horny.

Right now, that is.

"Your scent has changed." Kanuz drapes an arm across my shoulders, pulling me into him. "Do not be afraid, Gen. I am here."

"Yeah, but what the fuck is in *there*?" Knowing this temple, it could be a prehistoric snake. A megalodon. A nightmare.

"Are you afraid of swimming? Of water?" He puffs his chest out, side-eying me. "I can swim well enough for the both of us, my princess."

"No," I say, and I'm not. "I'm actually a fantastic swimmer, thank you very much, Captain Condescending."

"I am a prince, not a captain," he retorts.

And just like that, I'm smiling again. Still less than thrilled about getting in the stupid ass dark water, but his little misunderstandings are… endearing.

"It's just something humans say," I explain, then stop short. The water ripples. Bubbles burst at the surface.

Big bubbles.

"That could be from the shaking, right? Like…something in there is loose. Right?"

"Perhaps," Kanuz answers. He cocks his head, watching the water, and I relax against him slightly. "It is more likely there is something in there," he adds.

"Fuck." I eye the water. "What do you think we have to do? You're the expert. God, I wish I had a weapon, I hate this."

"I am your weapon," Kanuz tells me earnestly, and my heart does that little squeeze.

"I appreciate that," I say, because I do, "but I would feel better if I had my gun. Or an energy weapon. Whatever it is you Suevans like."

He holds up his talons.

"Right."

"We use energy weapons as well," Kanuz says with a hint of a laugh. "I will find one for you as soon as we are able to." He tugs me closer to him, and for a moment, I simply breathe him in, letting his now-familiar masculine, earthy smell wash over me.

It calms me, my heart slowing. It's probably just because I'm breathing slowly… but he *does* smell nice.

More bubbles appear.

"What would make those?" I ask conversationally, eyeing a skull-sized rock. Swimming with a rock is probably not my brightest idea.

"Probably a zeloth. They are very cute when they are small."

"Oh." Relief washes over me. "That's good to hear."

"They are deadly when they are full-grown, and I imagine the one that might make its home here is ancient."

"Oh." I swallow hard. "So… we're in trouble."

"It could be the rocks shifting, as you hypothesized." He shrugs, and pain flickers over his face.

"Why don't you let me look at where you're hurt?"

"Because there is nothing to do about it."

"Sure there is—"

"Our best bet is to keep moving, as you remind me every time you become aroused. If you did not keep telling me you are uninterested in exploring my sexual prowess, I would think you were in a hurry to bed me, Gen."

I huff an indignant breath.

Water surges upward, and my jaw drops as a wave drenches me.

"Oh, *shit*."

The thing that surfaces is, like everything on Sueva, huge. Tentacles flail, and as one slams into the rocky ground beside me, I note that the suckers are lined with what looks like tiny teeth. It's near translucent, blue veins and muscle visible underneath the clear skin. One giant eye protrudes from the sharp tip of a bulbous squid-like head.

"Lovely," I mutter.

"A zeloth," Kanuz proclaims, laughing a little as he shoves me behind him.

"Is it an ancient one?" I ask, suddenly yelling over the splashing of water and the strange squelching and clicking noises the creature's making. "It's pretty big!"

"No, my sweet golden flower, this is a medium-sized one." And with that, Kanuz laughs again, then swan dives into the black pool of water, disappearing under the thrashing tentacles.

Perfectly rational behavior.

When confronted with a big ole alien tentacle monster, laugh and dive in the water and take a nice swim with it.

Why not?

CHAPTER
FOURTEEN

KANUZ

THIS IS LESS THAN IDEAL. My tail propels me through the water, toward where the zeloth's most sensitive. The water is dark, yes, but not too dark to see. For my sweet wife, though, it must be terrifying. I set my jaw. There is nothing to do but move on and escape this place. I slice through the water, dodging to avoid a flailing arm of the great water beast.

Still, I cannot help but echo my mate's thoughts.

I wish I had a better weapon.

Sure, the zeloth is not as huge as I feared, but it is still a formidable opponent. To take it down, I will have one opportunity to strike its delicate underbelly. They cannot live out of the water, but I would not risk my Gen to lure it out onto dry land. I have to do this right.

If I miss, it will latch on to me and feast on my blood.

Even my hide is no match for its many knife-sharp teeth.

I hate to think of what the zeloth will do to my prickly but delicate mate. The thought spurs me forward, bubbles leaking from my nostrils as I careen towards my target.

There.

The soft, pale blue underbelly. I stretch my hand out, preparing to rake my talons across it, eviscerating it in one blow. I kick, closing in. One inch. A half inch.

Something wraps around my ankle, and I yell, the water swallowing the sound. As the creature tows me under, all I can think of is my sweet mate, and how I have failed her.

———

Gen

I pace the shoreline, the zeloth or tentacle monster or whatever preoccupied with Kanuz's ill-advised swimming lesson. Tentacles smash across the surface, and I don't bother dodging. I'm drenched. In fact, the displaced water laps at my ankles.

My eyes widen, and I look down.

Oh, *fuck* me. My heartbeat speeds up, and I can feel the adrenaline kicking into overdrive, sending tingles down my fingertips.

It's not displaced water.

The water is fucking *rising*. As I watch, open-mouthed, it surges past the tops of my boots.

"*Fuck* me."

A hoarse swear interrupts my reverie at this new shit-stain of a situation, and when I look up, the goddamn monster's holding Kanuz up by an ankle, blood leaking into the frothy water.

"The water's rising," I yell at him.

"Go for its underbelly," Kanuz shouts back, his eyes wild.

"Oh, so *now* you want to include me in your death-defying behavior?" I mutter, looking around for something, *anything*, I can use as a weapon. It better be death-defying. I don't want anything to happen to Kanuz. I don't want to do this alone.

I need him to be okay.

"Hang in there," I yell, ransacking my mind for a solution. The water continues to rise, way too fast. Fuck, fuck, fuckity fuck.

"What else would I do?" Kanuz responds, growling as he slashes at the tentacle holding him aloft. For a moment, I stand stock-still, unable to do anything but watch as he severs the tentacle. When he crashes into the water, my body unlocks, and I splash around like a chicken with its head cut off before settling on a sharp-edged rock.

Better than nothing.

My boots slosh as I move, the water nearly to my knees. They're going to weigh me down. Fuck. I put the rock down, unlacing my waterlogged boots as fast as I can. They float where I abandon them, and I work at the wet button to my pants, losing those too. I need to move as quickly as I can if I have a snowball's chance in hell of finding the tentacle monster's underbelly.

I didn't even know tentacle monsters had bellies, but here I am, in alien hell, learning all kinds of new, fucked-up shit!

Clad in my underwear, I shiver as the water hits my thighs, grabbing the sharp rock from where I've left it. The current of the rushing water tugs at my legs, pulling me backward, but I grit my teeth and push through to where Kanuz disappeared into the dark depths.

"Fuck the Federation," I grit out, furious and pumped up with adrenaline. "Fuck them for doing this to us." The alien monster makes a strange wet-sounding scream, and I glare at it. "And fuck you, too!"

I take another step forward, and my bare foot lands on nothing.

I'm in too deep now. I snort, then fill my lungs with air, and plunge into the abyss.

Cold water rushes all around me, and I open my eyes, trying to get my bearings. It's pitch black at first. But as I swim deeper, narrowly avoiding the tentacles, which seem occupied with Kanuz, definitely the bigger threat of the two of us, something blinks brightly deep, deep down.

A tentacle lashes at me, and bubbles burst from my mouth as it tears at my leg. I don't bother looking back, pushing deeper and away from the pain, away from the thrashing water above. The little lights below beckon, and I swim faster, my ears popping and lungs starting to burn.

Fish. It's little white fish, all glowing, as they flit around a circular object… bubbles stream from my mouth, and I try to make out the sculpture carved underground.

A serpent, slithering up a tree. No, not a tree. I swim as close as I dare, my brain yelling at me to breathe, as I try to get a better look.

It's a fucking handle. It's a water release valve.

It's a sluice gate.

Holy shit. Hope wells in me, and I kick my legs as hard as I can, dots dancing before my eyes with the need for air. It takes much too long to reach the surface, and I cough as I suck as much air in as I can.

"Gen, get its underbelly!" Kanuz shouts at me, still battling the thing.

"There's a door under there," I scream. "I'm going to open it."

"Good, yes, my brilliant flower, do that."

"Don't die!" I shout at him, noting in a rising panic that he's bleeding from several deep lacerations.

"I will not die before I have claimed you," he says dramatically.

"My hero," I tell him, and I'm not even sure if I'm being sarcastic. I'm pretty impressed with him, to be honest. I start hyperventilating, trying to flood my blood stream with oxygen. Hopefully the Suevan goddess didn't fucking rust the damn valve, or her little pet tentacle monster is going to have a nice dinner.

Okay. I can't put it off any longer. I take one last gulp of sweet cave air, and I swim as fast as I fucking can, heading for the sluice gate. The glowing fish dart around me, unbothered, and my ears pop as I yank at the gate. Nothing happens. Shit. That's not working.

I blow out a controlled stream of air, my face twisting as I strain at the door. Nothing.

"Fuck," I mutter, losing more air as the water swallows the word. Stupid.

I twist the handle this time, bracing my feet against the stone floor. A muffled clicking noise interrupts the rushing of water.

The sluice gate gives.

I twist more, relief and need to be out of this goddamn pool overriding every cell in my body screaming for more air. My thighs burn, the metal tearing my palms where I grip the bar, and *heave*, throwing my weight against it.

Might be easier if I were Suevan, but I'm a human, and I'm still gonna fucking do this thing.

When it swings open, I am unprepared for the shift in the current.

Stupid, stupid, idiot sandwich.

The gate grinds all the way open, and I'm immediately sucked into the opening, my chest burning with the need to breathe, my brain yelling at me to keep my fucking mouth and nose shut.

Water rushes around me so fast that I squeeze my eyes shut, crossing my arms over my chest and holding on to myself for dear life. Guilt tugs at me just as hard. Kanuz. I want to sob, but I'm too afraid to drown, so I simply hug myself.

My head breaks through the surface.

I gasp in a lungful of delicious oxygen, and this time, I let myself sob. Relief and fear both pound through me, and I can't stop crying. I'm alive. Kanuz is… not here.

I look back, trying to figure out how to get back to him, taking stock of where I am.

Stone walls rise up around me, barely visible through a dense crush of verdant foliage. The water continues to spill around me, up to my waist, but I'm sitting in it, mud thick around where I press my palms into it. Birds call to each other from the treetops, and in the distance, I can hear a fucking dinosaur.

Some kind of courtyard?

I stand slowly, still dizzy, exhausted from the rush of adrenaline leaving my body. I'm still crying, though the intensity of it has faded, leaving me whimpering as I trudge back through the muddy bank, searching for wherever it was the torrent of water carried me from.

"Kanuz, please be okay," I say, crying openly, rubbing my palms against my arm. Mud cakes my feet and ankles, and still I walk, to where water flows freely through a huge pipe. It's still coming so fast. There's no way I can swim through it to get to him.

Numb, I stand and watch it flow, waiting for a flash of green in the frothy blue, some hint of his skin.

But only water keeps rushing through, and another sob wracks me as I watch it flow.

"Kanuz, I don't want to do this without you," I choke out, my hand at my throat. "I need you with me, you have to be okay. Please, please don't be dead. I need you, you smug, funny, handsome alien prince." Tears stream down my face, and I hiccup, the water finally slowing. "I'm sorry I've been mean. I'm sorry. Please just come out of there. Alive."

A hand clasps on my shoulder, and I scream.

"My flower, I did not know you thought I was handsome." His voice is smug, but I'm too relieved to care.

I throw myself at him, sniffling as I wrap my arms around his broad chest as best I can. "You're here, you're okay," I say, and I'm not sure if I'm reassuring him or myself.

"You solved another riddle, my sweet flower. And you have not been mean." He pulls away, drinking in my face. "You have been yourself, in a rough situation. You have been a soldier, and a warrior princess, and a fine companion. Plus, you are very nice to look at."

I throw my cheek against his chest, suddenly crying harder.

"Why do you make water?" he asks earnestly, and I hiccup a laugh. "Are you ill? Did you drink too much of it?"

"It's called crying, and it's perfectly normal for humans," I tell him, amused. "We do it when we're sad. Or happy. Or angry. When we have a lot of emotions."

"I am sorry I have caused you so many emotions." He tilts his head. "Which one do you say you feel the most?"

I snort. "I'm relieved. I'm so happy you are okay."

"I like this crying, then. I am relieved we are both well." His arms curl around my bare skin, and I tense for a second, remembering I'm in nothing but underwear, then relax, hugging him tighter.

His body goes taut under my hands.

"Are you hurt?" Gingerly, I step away from him, or try to, but he pulls me back.

"The zeloth inflicted several wounds, but none are serious."

I inspect him, raking my gaze over his hide. He's bleeding from several places, but nothing looks too deep, thank goodness.

"You bleed, too," Kanuz says, his expression darkening. His hand slips down my hip, down the expanse of my thigh, to a laceration about two inches long. It seeps blood, but it's not deep. A purple bruise is already raised around the edges of the wound, though. Even his gentle inspection makes me wince.

"We're alive." I hang my head back, exhausted. "I was starting to wonder if I'd ever see the sky again. What happened to the monster?"

"The zeloth?"

"No, the other monster," I say, then grin. "Yes, the zeloth."

"It died when over half of it was exposed to the air. Immediately." He frowns. "It was deeply unpleasant to witness."

I am so fucking glad he's alive, and I can't stop myself from throwing my arms back around him.

"Perhaps I should fight zeloth more often, if this is the reaction I will receive." His voice is husky, and a hard mass prods against my bare leg.

I want to laugh, but it dies in my throat.

Maybe it's the near-death experience. Maybe it's the overwhelming relief at seeing him alive, his smug smirk firmly in place. Maybe it's because, if I listen to the little voice deep inside, I know I like him.

Really like him.

So with all the emotions tumbling inside me until they're polished and shiny, I do the only thing possible.

I tug his big, handsome face down to mine and kiss him like I mean it.

And I do.

CHAPTER
FIFTEEN

KANUZ

HER KISS STEALS my breath more surely than any threat of danger ever has. My relief at seeing her whole and alive is eclipsed by my affection for her. Need rages through me, the need to rut my mate until all the terrors of the past days are forgotten, until the world contracts and is only her and me, forever.

Her mouth is firm on mine, insistent, needy, and though my wounds throb gently, they will not stop me from taking anything she offers.

From taking everything she offers.

A growl rises in my throat as her tongue flicks against mine. My hands skate across her soft hips, the lean muscles in her stomach, until they stop at her rib cage, where her breasts are caged by thin, stretchy material.

As though she can read my thoughts, her hands press mine down. For a moment, regret fills me, that she won't allow me to touch her, that we will stop at these fervent kisses and nothing more.

Until her fingers find the edge of the material, and she tugs it up, over her shoulders, tossing it behind me.

I cannot tear my gaze away from her. "Gen-eveeve," I breathe, saying her full name.

Her blue eyes are full of fire, and she takes my hands, guiding them over her full breasts. They are soft, and luscious, and the perfect handfuls. I groan, harder than ever.

"You are so perfect," I tell her, bending down and lowering my head to her pretty pink nipple. I flick my tongue against it, and she gasps, the sound sending lightning through my veins. Her fingers curl through my hair, blunt fingernails scraping my scalp. I groan, my eyes half-closed, as I tug the delicate nipple into my mouth, sucking lightly.

"Kanuz," she moans, and the sound of her pleasure, of the hot need in her voice, is the most incredible thing I have ever heard.

My grip on her waist tightens, and I lick her nipple, the scent of her desire clouding my thoughts. All I want is to hear her lose herself, to watch as her eyes grow hazy with pleasure, to hear her say my name as she comes on my tongue.

I switch to the other breast, and she huffs a shaky breath as my fingertips replace my mouth.

"Kanuz," she says again, and I wrap my arm more fully around her, supporting her weight as she melts under my ministrations. Her skin is so soft. Every sigh of pleasure is a gift.

"What is it, my flower?" I ask her, then lick her sensitive nipple.

"I want to see if you're as good as you say you are." There's no hesitation in her voice, and I cannot help the wide grin that spreads across my face at her boldness.

"I am glad you are not shy, my princess. I want to hear you tell me everything you want. I want you to hear you beg for it."

"You have the dirtiest mouth. It's driving me crazy."

I pause, flummoxed, and look up at her. "My mouth is clean."

Laughter bursts out of her, the sound so light and musical it makes my heart soar.

"No, no, it means I like the way you talk."

"My words are dirty?"

"No." She gives her head an emphatic shake. "I really like how you talk to me. A lot."

I inhale deeply, and the proof of her words sings through me. "Then let me tell you this, my Gen. I would feast upon your cunt until all you can do is whimper, because words have lost their meaning. We would need no translators." I pause, running my finger down her stomach. She shudders as my talon hooks the edge of the small garment blocking her cunt from me.

"We would need no translators," I continue, "because all that would matter is how wet you are. How tight you'll be around my cock. How good it will feel when you come all around me."

"Oh, yes," she says, her eyes dark with lust, her body pliant against mine. "Let's put that dirty mouth to the test."

I growl, ripping the piece of fabric down the center. "I like all your challenges. I like all your edges. I like how underneath your prickles, you have a soft, kind heart." I drop to my knees, ripping her garment.

The flimsy material falls away, and my mate is bared to me, her scent even stronger now. I clutch her to me, savoring her. Savoring the soft, silken skin of her stomach against my cheek. The surprising curly hair that covers her here. The delicious smell of her, so mouthwatering I can take it no more.

I grip her hips, raising her up as she squeals. "Spread your legs for me, like a good wife," I command, and she groans, doing as I bid.

Her legs fall apart, and I raise her muscled body up until her legs fall across either shoulder. She squeals as I lick down the seam of her body.

"You are delicious," I tell her. "You are already wet and ready for me, Gen. Have you been this wet the whole time? Have you been this ready to be bred every time I look at you?"

"Kanuz," she whimpers, her fingers gripping my hair tight, squirming as I breathe against her glistening pink cunt. "Please, please."

"You are so polite like this," I tell her, my arousal painfully hard now, precum dripping from the tip, soaking into my pants. "Maybe I should make you straddle my face more often. I like it when you beg so nicely."

"Then please, *please* do it again."

I cock my head, enjoying the tight quality to her voice, the way her whole body is tight against mine, her thick, muscular ass in my hands. Her upper body curves over my head, and I slowly lower myself to the ground, so that she's seated on my face.

She raises up slightly, her chest heaving, but I yank her back down.

"You asked so nicely, my Gen, now enjoy your reward. You say that human females can come more than once, right? I will make you come until you cannot take it anymore."

"Oh, Kanuz," she moans, her fingers scrabbling against my skin.

I lick her sweet flesh, teasing her, listening to her gasps and cries as I run my tongue all over her cunt. There is a small nub at the top of her pretty pink slit, and she seems to like it best when I make small circles around it, teasing it.

When I suck it hard, she nearly jumps away from my face, groaning. Juices drench my mouth and chin, and I lap them up greedily. Her legs begin to shake, and I grin against her cunt as I continue to tease her, thrusting my tongue in and out of her body.

"Did you enjoy that, my little human?"

"Yes," she says, her body going taut again.

My need for her blazes higher still. I lift her off my face and onto my stomach. She lets out a little moan, writhing against me.

"I want you, Gen," I tell her. "I want you badly." I search her face, expecting her to deny me. Hoping she doesn't.

"I want it, too," she tells me, her cheeks flushed as pink as her swollen cunt. "I want you, Kanuz."

There's an unexpected sweetness to her words, and it sends me past the edge of control. The tightly leashed restraint I've choked myself with the past few weeks snaps. Growling, I grip her hips, and she cries out, wide-eyed, as I roll her to the ground, throwing her legs wide open.

My pants can't come off fast enough, and I grunt in frustration as she rubs her hand down my hardness.

"My laces are too wet."

"Let me," she says. Her gaze rakes over my cock, and it sets me on fire. Undone by it, I hold her face in my hands, claiming her mouth in a savage kiss. She opens her mouth to me, so pliant and greedy I nearly spill early.

I cannot resist this female.

And I no longer have to.

CHAPTER
SIXTEEN

GEN

THIS IS THE *BEEEEST!*

The prince did not tell a single lie, no he did not! I'm flying on the wings of one of the best orgasms in the history of orgasms, so fucking happy my alien is alive and well I can't even stand it.

Kanuz kisses the daylight out of me, and I taste myself on his tongue, which makes me even hotter for my slab of scaly muscles. The knot on his pants finally comes undone, and I pull away from his kiss, tugging his sodden pants off as fast as I can.

He laughs, and it's a dark sound, full of promise. It sends a fresh shiver through me, and he pulls his pants the rest of the way off, his huge cock swinging free.

I swallow, eyeing it slightly warily.

I mean, it makes sense that it's massive, considering my alien is close to seven feet tall, and I'm no stranger to dicks, but this one is... big. And bumpy. And there's a thing sitting above it *vibrating.*

Curious, I reach out, stroking my hand across it.

Oh, yeah, it's vibrating, all right.

"That is my xof. It readies our females to be ripened." His

voice is tight, and sure enough, when I glance up at him, his eyes are squeezed shut.

A smirk climbs across my face, and I run my fingers over it lightly again. His cock jerks, white fluid beading at the top. It's sensitive, all right.

"You think to tease me?" he rasps.

"I—" My words fail as he raises his fingers to his mouth, biting off two talons cleanly.

My eyes go wide as I realize what he's about to do.

"I promised you as many orgasms as your human body will allow," he tells me, one hand braced against my chest, pushing me back into the ground.

His other hand spreads my legs wide, and then his dark head dives between my legs, his rough tongue running all along my already sopping pussy.

"Oh, Kanuz," I groan, his thick, blunted finger entering me.

"You are so tight," he tells me, his voice thick. His tongue swipes across my clit, and I cry out, overstimulated and already on the edge again. "You are going to feel so fucking good around my cock."

"I want that," I say, practically sobbing as he sucks my clit, adding a second finger inside me.

"Tell me again," he growls, the words resonating against my core.

"I want you deep inside me, Kanuz, now," I'm begging, spun up on need and lust and a warmth towards this male that I would never have thought possible.

"Fuck," he murmurs. "You taste so good." His tongue darts out again, and I arch off the ground, burying my hands in his thick black hair, pulling his head closer still.

I'm grinding shamelessly against his face, and he picks up the rhythm I set, licking and sucking and nibbling until I'm so goddamn close—

And then he stops, pulling his fingers out of me with a wet, sloppy sound as I moan in desperation.

"I can't wait any longer," he says.

"Yes," I moan, needing to be filled, feeling so empty and close and then he's there, his huge head pushing at my entrance.

"Relax," he growls, his newly shorn nails teasing over my clit. His mouth covers mine, swallowing the animalistic noises erupting from me, his fangs pressing against my lips, so different and so right.

He thrusts his hips forward slowly, his cock slipping further inside, inch by inch. Kanuz trails kisses down my jawline and neck, and I shiver, my legs shaking.

His xof vibrates so hard I can feel it as he enters me, and then he groans, thrusting hard, and I cry out as he seats himself fully inside me.

We stare at each other for a long moment. His xof vibrates harder, and I moan, my eyes wide, as it stimulates my clit.

"Are you ready, my flower?" he asks, and the question is so sweet, so full of unexpected worry, that affection sweeps through me.

"Yes," I breathe.

He doesn't move though, not yet. Instead, he stares down at me, his gaze full of wonder. He raises one hand up, tracing a finger across my jawbone.

"I must be the luckiest male alive, to have one such as you."

My heart skips, and I smile up at him. I'm about to say something else, when he *moves*, and any rational thoughts disappear.

Oh. My. God.

The bumps. The vibrating. My hands fly to his hips, and my eyes roll back in my head. So much sensation.

So good. My body quakes, and I raise my hips to meet each thrust. He's so tall that my head's at his chest, but he curls down, kissing me softly and staring into my eyes as he picks up the pace.

"Feels so good," I say, completely lost in the overwhelming surge of feeling. I wrap my arms around his waist, running my fingernails down his back, savoring every muscle, every ripple of power.

"You are everything," he groans, "*everything*. You are mine, do you understand me?"

"I understand," I whine, his xof driving me higher and higher.

"Tell me you're mine," he demands, his pace savage and fast.

I wrap my legs around him, nudging my feet into him, so close again I'm nearly out of my mind with pleasure. "Yours, Kanuz, yours."

"My princess," he says, and the words are victorious.

When he kisses me again though, it's tender and soft, and it doesn't feel like a loss, not at all.

I fall apart with a cry as his tongue sweeps across mine, his fingers tweaking my nipple as I shudder beneath him.

He comes a moment later with a brutal thrust, and I can feel it —his cum hot, searing through me.

I cry out again, the feeling winding me tight and loose all over again.

Finally, I slump, my legs quaking, and he pulls me tight against him.

"Now sleep, Princess." His fingers comb through my hair, and for once, I don't have a comeback. It's all too easy to fall asleep in his arms, safe, the Suevan sky overhead.

CHAPTER
SEVENTEEN

KANUZ

I HAVE NEVER FELT SO whole in my life, as I do with this delicate golden female slumbering beside me. I hardly dare take breath, too afraid of disturbing her.

All I want is to watch her sleep, watch the delicate fluttering of her eyelids, the lax shape of her addictive mouth. The plump curves of her breasts and the muscled thighs. One leg's draped over me, and my cock's hard again, still inside my sleeping mate.

It feels so fucking good.

Our scents mingle together now, and it heightens my desire for her. I want to mate her, fuck her, until there is only us. No fear scent, nothing but our shared pleasure.

There will never be enough where Gen is involved.

My princess.

My mate.

Finally. *Finally*. I frown, my gaze wandering past the treasure in my arms to the temple courtyard, overgrown with vegetation.

I do not know what the puzzle will be here, but I do not doubt this place is chock full of challenges. I hope on the asteroids above that the many-faced-goddess will take mercy on my mate and me. I hope that we are through the worst of it.

I long to have her safe and sound and well pleasured in my bed, not sprawled on the ground covered in muck, hungry and exhausted.

This is no way for a princess to be treated.

It is no way to treat a treasure at all.

When the moons are heavy in the sky, I finally close my eyes, somewhat assured that we will find no trouble this night, at least.

———

My eyes fly open.

Beside me, Gen stirs in her sleep, restless. I pause, frowning. The night is almost over, orange and red breaking across the sky as the sun blazes into view. A bush rustles nearby, and I tense, on high alert, only to relax again as a bird flies from the brush.

Gen cries out next to me, her feet slamming into my shins.

"No, don't," she pants, the words thick with sleep. Her fingers move, all her muscles twitching. "I can't. Don't."

"Gen," I say, shaking her shoulder, alarmed.

"Don't fucking touch me," she screams, her eyes squeezed tight.

"Gen, my princess, it's Kanuz. You're safe." I wince. Safe enough, at the moment. "Wake up."

She inhales deeply, her bare chest heaving. Slowly, her muscles calm, and her eyes blink open.

"What's wrong?" she asks blearily.

"You were having a bad dream," I tell her, pulling her closer to me, now that I'm not worried she'll kick me in the xof.

"I was," she says, her face falling, her gaze going distant. "I was dreaming about the invasion." Her breath hiccups. "Did I wake you? I'm sorry."

"No," I tell her, nuzzling the nape of her neck, drinking her in. "Do not apologize."

She snuggles closer, throwing an arm over my neck. I like her like this—sleepy and loose-limbed, soft and sweet. I like her in all moods. She's a summer day, golden sunshine and humor, hot sun and passion, a sudden storm breaking in the afternoon, the warm night holding close in a dark embrace.

"Do your dreams trouble you often?" I ask her, worried. Worried, and furious at the Roth, for all my impotent wrath will do to help her now. If I see another Roth ever again, I'll rip their spine out and give it to her as a gift.

"I mean, it's not a big deal," she says softly, her voice already thick with sleep again. I have run my poor mate ragged.

"It is to me." I smooth her hair away from her face, luxuriating in her presence.

"It's over. It's over," she repeats, and I wonder if she's telling me, or if she's simply reassuring herself.

I hate them even more for what they did to her, and for what they did to her people. What they did to Suevans and the other species at our settlements was terrible, but we had the technology and numbers to repel them.

The humans were sorely outclassed.

And here is the outcome of it: my sweet Gen, lax with sleep beside me, sold into our marriage by a government who would do anything to stop the Roth from attacking again.

At least I know our shipment is well on its way to Earth.

"I will not allow it to happen again, my love," I tell her, holding her tighter.

She sighs against me.

"I vow it on the goddess herself. I will not allow the Roth to ravage another planet like they did Earth."

A flock of birds flings itself into the dawn sky, silhouetted black against the rising sun.

I tuck my Gen under my chin and watch them fly, wishing we could sprout wings and do the same, so that my female could be safe.

I cannot fail her again. I cannot be the reason she wakes in the night, screaming her fears into the dark.

I will not allow it.

Sleep finally claims me again, but it's restless despite the blessed female in my arms.

When we wake again, the sun's hot in the sky above.

Gen stretches long, yawning and blinking. A sheen of sweat dots her brow, and she sits up slowly, rubbing her neck.

"Why are you staring at me?" she asks, shoving my shoulder playfully. At least, I think it's playful. Maybe it is a hard shove for her.

"Because you are the most miraculous thing I have ever seen."

Her cheeks flush pink, and a low growl slips out of my throat. "When you turn that color, it makes me ravenous for you. For all your parts that are that same color."

She gives me a coy smile, her arm crossed over her chest, hiding her breasts from me.

"Do not hide those."

"I need to find my bra."

"Is that what you call it?"

She tilts her head at me. "You don't have that word? It's like…" She jiggles her breasts, and my cock immediately stands at attention. "It holds them down. Keeps them from bouncing around, you know? It hurts when they move too much."

"I like when they move," I say, only half-paying attention to what she's said.

A small laugh ripples out of her, her cute furry eyebrows darting upward. "I'm sure you do. But if we have to run… it doesn't feel good."

"I want you to feel good," I say sincerely.

"Me too, dude." Sighing, she stands, then her eyes go wide as she looks back at me. "You ripped my underwear off. I have no panties."

"Does that—" I motion to her cunt. "—hurt when you run, too?"

Her cheeks suck in, an expression I now recognize as her trying not to laugh "No. No, it doesn't, but I don't want to be completely naked in the jungle."

"Completely naked?" I stare at her for a long second, then remember how I found her. Leaking water and crying, wearing only the tiniest scraps of fabric. "What happened to your shoes? You cannot run in the jungle without shoes."

"I don't have a massive tail, Kanuz. They would have weighed me down in the water. My pants, too. Surviving in the moment seemed smarter than bringing all that shit with me."

I blow out a breath, frustrated at myself all over again for putting her in this situation, where she had to choose between nudity and survival. Not that I am upset she is nude.

No, quite the opposite.

But her skin is too fragile to be exposed to the elements, and her little feet will surely be hurt by stepping on things.

"I am sorry," I tell her, my heart heavy.

"Why? You didn't summon that giant tentacle monster. You didn't drop me here and *force* me to marry you."

My fangs bite into my lower lip, my molars grinding together at her words. "Is that how you feel?"

Sure, I know now that she was, in fact, tricked into marrying me, and as reprehensible as that is, I am a prince. I am handsome, and I brought her pleasure and smiles.

My stomach sinks.

"Kanuz, wait, I like you. A lot. I was… terrified that something happened to you." Her words turn thick, her eyes welling with more emotion water. "But yeah, I was forced here under false pretenses. I'm not going to lie to you about that to make you feel better."

I stand and walk over to where my pants lie in a clump on the ground. "Here," I say, my voice rough and gravelly. "Take mine."

"Kanuz, stop." Her expression is pained, and I long to soothe her, to rub it away with kisses.

But she's right. She is completely correct. She was *forced* to marry me, tricked by her own people. And I have taken advantage of her most cruelly. Her survival was dependent upon me, and now?

Now all she wants is to cover her body.

The least I can give her is that.

"Kanuz, they're going to be huge," she says. "And don't. Don't act like that."

"I am not acting like anything."

"You're being weird." She purses her lips, her eyes welling with water again. "Is it because we had sex?"

I want to tell her no. But of course, she is right. It is because we had sex. Because I took something that she wasn't ready to give. She might have said yes, but she didn't say yes to being my wife… nor my mate.

Nausea turns my stomach. "Put on the pants, Gen."

She sniffs, and my heart aches as I realize she's leaking water from her eyes again. "What happened to being your flower?" Her voice is tight, and shock jolts through me as I realize I've hurt her.

Which means… she *does* like me. And I'm pushing her away.

"I am being an idiot lunch." I sigh, rubbing my neck.

Gen sniffs, then laughs, wiping her eyes with her hands. "Idiot sandwich." Her small hands clasp my larger ones, and the pants fall, forgotten, to the ground. "And yes, you are, Kanuz. I wouldn't have had sex with you if I didn't want to. And I did very much want to have sex with you. Would I have chosen to marry you after being in your august presence for five minutes? No, because I am not an idiot sandwich… And as awful as the last few weeks have been, you've been the only bright spot. You have kept us safe, and fed, and made me laugh more times than I can count. Don't push me away because I'm angry that the Federation took my choice away. It doesn't mean I'm not choosing *you* right now."

"I feel foolish," I admit. "I am sad that you did not choose to come here and be mine. But I understand your anger. Would you choose to marry me again? Now that you know me?"

She blows out a breath, tilting her chin up and staring me down in her frank, no nonsense way. "Out of all the males that were there, Prince Kanuz of Sueva, I am glad you chose me to be your princess and your wife."

It's not an answer, not really, but perhaps it was unfair for me to ask that of her.

So instead of pressing her more, I push down my sadness and draw her to me, kissing her firmly. She makes a small noise of pleasure, and I don't care if she would marry me or not.

Right now, in the temple of the many-faced-goddess, she has said she is mine.

And I will do with my mate as I please.

Starting with making her scream with pleasure, yet again.

"It seems to me that I did not keep my promise to you last night."

Gen stares up at me from heavy-lidded eyes. "What promise?"

"That I would make you come as many times as you could handle."

She squeals as I hoist her up, and I raise her high enough that I can capture the pink tip of her enticing breast. "I will never get enough of these. Of you, my golden flower." I stare at her, and she throws her arms around my neck, kissing the column of my throat. I do not have much feeling there, as my scales protect my neck, but I learned last night that she likes to be kissed there very much, so I do the same to her.

A sigh wends out of her, and she goes soft against me, her legs circling my waist. Her hands cup my face, and my heart aches at the beautiful trust etched on her face. My prickly princess has come so far.

And it only took days of terrible ordeals to get her to trust me. I sigh wearily.

"I have not pampered you as I should have," I tell her.

"Please. I'm a military officer in the Earth Federation. Or—" she pauses, looking slightly lost. "I was. Regardless, I don't need to be pampered."

"It is not about need. It is about what you deserve." I kiss her cheek bone, where it pinkens under the slight pressure from my lips, then the tip of her nose, then the other cheek, and finally her mouth. "I want to take you again, Gen, but I think for now? I will simply pamper you as you deserve before we move on."

"Oh, is that right, Tarzan? And what are you planning on pampering me with around here?" A lyrical laugh trickles out of her. "Lemme guess: mud baths. Clay masks. Salt scrub. Hot stone massage."

I shake my head, not understanding her strange string of words. "Are these things humans do? Does Indiana Jones do a hot stone massage?"

She laughs again, the sound vibrating through her chest into mine. I hold her more closely, enjoying being near her. Her happiness is like bathing in the sunlight.

I step back, still clutching her tight against me. A burbling stream runs through the overgrown courtyard here, and I walk along the bank, holding my Gen all the while. She smiles at me, looking around curiously with her big blue eyes.

"What is this place?"

"I do not know, not exactly, but I assume it is one of the places where they would worship the goddess, a long time ago."

"Are there many places like this on Sueva? This is so magical."

It hits me then, that she does not know anything about our planet. Our people. Not really. We've been surviving in the jungle for two weeks now, and she has seen nothing of Sueva save for the small village we had her crew debark at for counter intelligence's sake.

"This temple is very, very old, but if you mean to ask whether there are places where nature and people live in harmony, then the answer is yes. We respect the goddess, who is everywhere in Sueva. The city of Edrobaz, where our First Warlord Draz rules, is full of myza."

"Myza?"

"Houses in trees," I clarify. "Edrobaz is one of a kind, a city in the clouds at the top of a mountain."

"Oh, wow," she breathes, her eyes round and focused on me. "That sounds really cool."

"The temperature is steady, thanks to an atmospheric dome."

She grins, and I realize I've misunderstood the human slang word.

"Don't pout," she says, clucking her tongue and poking my bottom lip. "It's cute when you don't get it right away."

"I am a prince! I am not cute." I spit the last word, my mock rage making her laugh.

"Princes have to be cute. It's in the job description."

"And princesses must be beautiful warriors, so it looks like I chose perfectly." My tone is smug, and her grin widens.

"You know," she says, her fingers dancing along my shoulder. "I haven't liked to be called beautiful lately. It's been a long time since I liked hearing that. A very long time."

"Why is that?" I ask, stepping carefully around a weathered statue. I think I know the answer, but maybe it will help her to speak her truth. And what better place to speak truths than in the temple of the many-faced-goddess?

Her sigh is long, and she's silent for long enough while I walk that I think she will not answer.

"After the Roth came, everything changed. There wasn't room for being pretty. I didn't want to be pretty. Even trying made me feel silly and young and naïve. I saw firsthand what happened to the people they murdered, and there just wasn't a point to it after that." She lapses into silence, her expression contemplative, her fingers tapping a staccato beat against my scales.

I let the silence grow, my heart breaking for her all over again. This woman, she has been through so much. She had to grow a thick skin to hide her softness from the world. She had to be tough.

And now she opens up to me, just like the golden flower greets the morning sun, showing off the true treasure inside.

"It's nice," she says, her voice so quiet I have to strain to hear her. "It's nice to feel like maybe, with you, I can be both parts of me. I can let myself have pretty things, if we get to Edro—" She stumbles over the word.

"Edrobaz," I finish for her.

"If we get there, I can be both. I can be the Genevieve I used to be, and I can still be the new me. I can let myself enjoy things."

"It makes me sad to hear that you have not enjoyed things since the Roth invaded."

She makes clicking sounds with her tongue, her mouth pulling to the side as she stares at a patch of clouds beyond my head. "No, I did enjoy things. Just different things." She shrugs one shoulder, drawing my eye to the fetching way her breast moves. "I put aside things that weren't necessary. I enjoyed my work. I enjoyed learning to protect people. Protect myself."

"That is very honorable. You will be a wonderful princess."

Her legs clench around me, then loosen again. I narrow my eyes at her, pushing a branch of a tree out of our way.

"What? Do you not want to be a princess?"

"I mean, I already am, right?"

"That is not an answer." The mud squelching between my toes turns to stone, and I glance down in surprise. Ahead, the thick underbrush butting up against the stream fades away into a stone courtyard. A fountain lies in the center, a worn statue of the goddess in the middle, one palm raised toward the Suevan sky, water running from her other hand. It's so old that the likeness is barely recognizable, all features battered away by the constant exposure.

The fountain water runs clear and clean, however, a testament to the knowledge and prowess of the Suevan ancestors.

"Here we are, my Gen," I tell her. "Now I can pamper you thoroughly."

"I do love to bathe," she says, her white teeth flashing in a smile. "That was something I never quite managed to give up."

"Here," I say, placing her on the edge. She immediately steps into the water, mud and dirt flaking away. She cups her hands, placing them under the spout and drinking deeply.

I step in beside her, kneeling at her feet and scrubbing gently at the mud that cakes her. There are cuts and bruises all over her skin.

"You are in bad shape, my love. Your poor fragile skin is battered."

She freezes, staring down at me. Surprise is written over every inch of her face. "What?"

"You are covered in cuts. Are you in pain?"

"N-no." Her lovely eyes are still wide, her brow pinched together. She stares at me as though I am a puzzle in need of solving.

"It does not hurt at all?" I ask, touching the wound from the zeloth.

She winces slightly. "No, it does hurt. Just not enough to complain about."

I tilt my head, looking around at the vegetation as though for the first time. "This was once a garden," I say slowly, realization dawning. "The priestesses that tutored me when I was young, they had a garden they kept as well. They taught me about the properties of many of our native plants. Ancestral healing plants."

"You think there are healing plants here?" she asks, understanding dawning across her face.

"There is a plant called dreza. When crushed, the leaves make a fine salve. It has healing properties that the priestesses attributed to the power of the goddess. I wonder if there are solman berries here, too."

"Food," my princess moans, and her stomach rumbles loudly.

"Stay here," I tell her, excited that I can at least soothe two of her immediate problems. We can both use the dreza salve and the nourishment from the berries, but I ache to ease her pain.

"Easy as pie," she responds, plonking down in the shallow water, gingerly rubbing at the remaining patches of mud and grime. I watch her for a moment, transfixed by the vision before me. My naked, bathing human. She sits in the white stone fountain, the water sparkling in the sunlight, a peaceful expression on her face, water streaming over her smooth skin.

She looks like she belongs here.

With me.

I will make her see it, too.

CHAPTER
EIGHTEEN

GEN

I LIKE THIS PLACE. Out of all the weird places on this planet, this one is by far my favorite. Water trickles over my shoulders as I lean my hair back into the clean water pouring from the statue's hand. It's cool, but with the sun beating down overhead, it's refreshing as opposed to shocking.

The overgrown garden, though it seems strange to even call it a garden, is beautiful and otherworldly. Huge white buds hang from thick vines climbing up tree trunks. Several plants are shades I've never seen on Earth, purple ferns with vibrant pink striping, deep sapphire leaved bushes studded with crimson many-petaled flowers. Winged bugs float over the flowers, a strange cross between dragonflies and butterflies.

And they're bioluminescent, glowing faintly when they dip into shade.

It's striking and surreal, quiet and calm, and peace sneaks over me.

I sigh so heavily that it's shaky, as though I've been sobbing for hours on end. It's like all the anxiety and stress departs my body in that one breath, leaving me with my thoughts.

He called me his love.

Not his princess, or his golden flower, or any of the other silly and sweet pet names he's bestowed on me.

His love.

My heart stutters at the mere thought, and I scan the foliage for him, wondering where he wandered off to. Not that I would see him, not with his coloring and the dappled light.

But I look for him still.

Part of me wonders if I'll ever stop looking for him. I bite my lip, rubbing water over my face.

Kanuz isn't the first to tell me he loves me.

But I think he might be the first to really mean it.

My toes curl underwater as memories of last night flash through my mind.

The prince certainly lived up to his own hype, and that's also a new first. I'm pleasantly sore, and everything throbs with the sudden desire zipping through me as my body remembers the way he felt inside me.

I sigh, leaning back against the pocked stone of the statue, and resume trying to clean the caked on mud off my toes and feet. No use mooning about like some lovestruck teen. My alien will be back soon, and with food.

A girl can't ask for much more than a good dicking down and some fresh fruit from the alien she loves.

I sit up quickly, water splashing all around me in my haste.

Wait.

Did I just... do I?

Do I *love* him?

Does the thought of being married, really being married to Kanuz, not just accidentally married, send warm fuzzies through me? My hand goes to my abdomen, and in the peaceful calm of the temple garden, I'm imagining it.

I'm imagining having his babies. Our babies.

A family.

A dream I thought the Roth stole from me all those years ago, roaring back full force. I never thought having kids was some kind of pinnacle goal for me, but it was something that was always there, as an option. Until Earth felt too dangerous to scrape by on my own, let alone bringing kids into the world.

I may not be safe here, in the jungle, but Kanuz is a huge, protective alien. He loves me.

He loves me.

The thought steals my breath. A winged insect darts to and from a patch of shade, glowing a luminous green.

This may not have been a life I ever imagined for myself... but I'm not sure I can imagine anything else.

My cheeks hurt. I touch my fingertips to my face. I'm grinning like a fool.

"A princess," I murmur, wriggling my toes. "I love him?" I add, and the sudden quickening of my heart makes me smile harder.

I think I do.

The only thing that could make this perfect is if I had my friends to gossip with about it. My crew.

My stomach growls. Okay, maybe food and some clothes would help, too. And a safe place to sleep, out of the Suevan wilds and this temple.

The crew. Gah, I miss them more than I thought possible. I let the water trickle over my hand, watching it spill from my fingertips, mimicking the statue overhead. What would Bex say if I told her I fell in love with an alien prince?

A small laugh erupts from me.

She would be dancing around excitedly, chaotic and full of energy as always, probably asking inappropriate and hilarious questions about Kanuz's package. I snort at the thought, practically hearing her voice in my head.

Still thirsty, I drink some more water. It's crisp and delicious and leaves me feeling sated and bubbly. Or maybe it's just finally seeing the open sky again.

"I hope my friends are all right," I say out loud. If Kanuz's goddess is real, maybe she's listening. Can't hurt to try and speak it into existence, regardless. I'm not huge on woo-woo stuff, but I have read my fair share of mind over body studies, mostly during the brutal training for Federation officers.

My lips twist to the side. I'm not sure I can speak hopes for my friends into existence.

"I hope we can leave the jungle safely," I amend. "I hope that what I have with Kanuz is real, and isn't some byproduct of being stuck surviving together. I hope that he doesn't get tired of me." I didn't realize it was something I was worried about until I said it out loud. There have been so many other, immediate concerns that that one wasn't even on my radar. But there it is, hanging outside my body now.

What if I'm just a passing novelty to him? What if I'm just one more alien female to bang?

"I want him to love me. Really love me," I say quietly, to no one at all. "I want to be what he thinks I am. I want to help his people, and Earth, too." I don't want to be mean Gen anymore, sarcastic and thorny and contrary. It's exhausting, being tough all the time.

I miss being able to let my guard down. With Kanuz, I feel like I finally can.

My nose wrinkles, and I stare down at my hands, which all but sparkle in the sunlight. I tilt my head. Weird. They look like they actually sparkle. I shake them, trying to dislodge the effect.

It doesn't budge.

Maybe I'm dehydrated. I wouldn't be surprised, not with as much physical activity as we've been doing. This water is like nothing else. It's freaking *delicious*.

I cup my hands, drinking from the now trickling water. Weird. Why has it stopped flowing? I scoot my naked butt around, making sure I'm not blocking the drain or something.

But no. There's no drain.

Confused, I stand. The water level's lower, without a doubt.

"I didn't drink *that* much." I wring my wet hair out, but the water's all but evaporated from it already. "What the fuck?"

My stomach lurches, and I stare down at my feet, which aren't just sparkling, but appear to be glowing.

Glowing. Glowing a bright, shimmery green, just like the insects flitting around.

"Oh god," I say, fear rippling through me. "It wasn't water."

I press my palm against my forehead. Maybe I'm feverish. Maybe this is a hallucination.

"My flower?" Kanuz's voice tears through the garden, and I turn immediately to him.

"Am I glowing?" My voice is frantic. "Please tell me I'm not hallucinating. Or that if I am, it's fine. That this is going to be fine. You can lie to me, Kanuz, I don't care."

"I cannot and will not lie to you, my Gen." His eyes are wide, his arms limp at his sides, the huge, folded leaf in his hand forgotten. He goes to his knees, gaze glued to me. "You are glowing. The goddess has given you her gift, the treasure of the temple."

"Shit," I say weakly.

"That is not the gift," he says. "You are the key, my love. You will unite Sueva."

"Why am I glowing?" I ask. "Am I going to get sick?" I can't even focus on what he's saying. I'm too worried about my new bioluminescence. "There has to be an explanation for this."

"You are the new symbol of a united Sueva," Kanuz tells me, ignoring my questions, his gaze rapt on my naked body. "And you are a human female. They will not be able to ignore the goddess' blessing now. Truly, my love, you are one of a kind."

"I'm glowing." I say again, stuck on that fact. "Why am I glowing?"

"There must be some sort of bioluminescent marker in that fountain."

"Is it safe?" I squeak. I don't want to be murdered by my own thirst. Real thirst, that is, not the lust I feel, staring at the big alien still on his knees in front of me.

Concern furrows his brow, and he stands, clutching the leaf to his chest. "We will find out. Do you feel ill?"

I pause, checking in with my body. "No?"

He beams at me, his smile contagious. "Then let us assume, for now, that you are safe. We will test you more extensively when we get back to civilization."

Kanuz closes the distance between us, still staring at me with an awed expression. I shift my weight, finally logging the words he said.

"I'm the symbol of a united Sueva," I repeat, uncertainty snaking through me.

"You are everything, my love." He places the leaf on the now dry fountain, catching me up in a hug.

"Do I get superpowers?" I shove at him, testing my strength. I wilt a little when he chuckles. "Apparently not."

"You already have them," he tells me, his voice thick with emotion. "You are kind, and strong, a true survivor. You have a heart of gold, that you keep locked away. But now you cannot hide it. You shine with your goodness."

"It sounds like a lot of responsibility," I croak.

He snorts. "Let us focus on the positive. We are finished with this temple. I found a tunnel exit while you were busy drinking the treasure. It's blocked by the roots of a gnarled zitsu tree, impossible to see from the outside. We are well outside the swamp entrance now, too. I think you will be pleased to hear that."

"Oh my god, we're free? We can leave?" I want to cry with relief. Instead, I bury my face in his chest, seeking comfort from my husband.

"We can, my love, we can." His hand strokes through my hair, his touch soothing and so, so right.

"Kanuz," I say, peeling myself off him and taking his face in my hands. "I love you." It comes out fierce and harsh, with none of the softness I expected.

"Of course, you do," he says arrogantly, his tail swishing

behind him. "I am your husband."

I can't help but laugh.

"And I love you, my goddess blessed treasure. Now, let us get the fuck out of here, as you would say, so that we can settle the dispute on this planet once and for all."

"Yeah," I yell, pumping my fist. Glowing sparks shoot from my hand as I raise it, and I stare at it in alarm. "You think that's going to wear off? That's excessive."

"No, I do not." He's downright cheerful about it. "Now, my glowing one, eat some of these berries I've foraged for you while we walk. Here." He dips his fingers in the gooey stuff leaking from the big leaf, and slathers it on my skin. "The dreza will soothe your wounds." He blows a cool breath over the salve, and it instantly seems to alleviate the aches. He smiles down at me. "Ready? If you prefer, I can carry you."

He doesn't give me the option, though, simply scooping my naked ass up, then tossing the leaf pouch full of berries on my stomach.

"Are they good?"

"Very good. They do not grow everywhere on Sueva."

I eye one. It looks almost like a blackberry, but not quite. "It's not going to poison me?"

He stops, aghast. "I would not give you poison berries."

"I'm human. You might not know what would hurt me."

"Do you not trust me, prickly star?"

"Can you settle on a damn pet name for me?" I gripe. "You're giving me whiplash." I pop a berry in my mouth, too hungry to worry about it. If Kanuz says it's safe, it's safe.

"No," he replies. "I like it too much when you scowl at me to stop."

I chew, the flavor exploding on my tongue. It's not bitter or gross like I would expect from something poisonous. It's tart to the point of sour, and then it melts away into surprising sweetness.

The light grows dim under the canopy of trees, and I keep

eating berries, enjoying every mouthful. Frankly, I'm not mad about being carried around, either. I'm fucking exhausted.

"You are glowing more now." His voice is full of wonder.

"It's darker here," I say through a mouthful of berries. "Thank you, by the way. These are delicious. They remind me of Sour Patch Kids."

He stops suddenly, and my head jerks. I cough on a half-swallowed berry.

"Humans eat their children?"

"What?!" Consternated, I stare up at him. "Why would you think that?"

"You said you eat kids. Children."

"Oh, oh. No. No! It's a type of candy."

"Can-dee?"

"Yeah, you know, sweets? It's a treat. Sugary and sour treat."

He starts walking again, juggling me to push foliage out of the way. "Why did you call it kids?"

"They're shaped like that."

"Your sweets are shaped like small children? Why?" His tone is completely confused and I can't help but laugh at the appalled expression on his face.

"Honestly, I have no idea. Marketing, I guess."

"Why would anyone think eating children is appealing? Truly, the more I learn about your species, the more I worry for them."

"Same, to be honest." I pop another handful of berries into my mouth. "I'm so glad we're getting out of here."

"It should be a day's journey to Edrobaz, where your crew awaits. And then we can begin the work of uniting Sueva."

"Can we rest first?" I ask, not at all embarrassed by how whiney the question is.

"My flower, do you have to ask? I have not even *begun* pampering you. Besides, my cock will not allow you to leave the bed for at least a week."

"That's... a long time." I make my face as serious as possible.

He squints down at me. "You can handle it," he assures me.

I crack up. I can't help it. Between whatever the fuck was in that water and the knowledge we're done with the temple, I'm effervescent with relief and happiness. We fall quiet as we reach the outer wall, and sure enough, a massive tree sprawls overhead. The leaves are twice the size of my body.

"Here," Kanuz says, gingerly placing me on the ground. "I do not think the tunnel is big enough for me to carry you safely, Princess."

"I can walk," I say, still eyeing the tree. "Can you grab me one of those?"

He cranes his neck up. "One of what?"

"One of those big leaves."

"Anything for the goddess blessed."

I raise an eyebrow, unsure if he's joking or not. Hopefully he is. That's a *little* much. Kanuz begins climbing the tree with ease, his talons biting into the bark. Muscles bunch under his scaley green hide, and I lick my lips, practically salivating at the site. Even his thick tail seems normal now, and he uses it to balance as he clings to the gargantuan trunk.

"Go, Kanuz," I cheer. "You're doing great." I raise a hand in the air, then sigh as little sparks twinkle off of it. "Wish this came with an off switch," I mutter.

Within a matter of minutes, Kanuz is back in front of me, hardly even out of breath.

"You made that look easy."

He tosses his hair back, waggling his brows at me. "That is because I am a prime specimen."

I laugh, and he holds out not one, but two torso sized leaves. "I can't say I've ever heard someone say that. Maybe it will catch on as a pick-up line."

He grins at me, and I take the leaves. "I guess we're just gonna Eve it. Not a fig leaf, but it'll do. I hope there aren't any devilish snakes around here." I wink at him, but he squints at me in confusion.

"Right." I shake my head. "You wouldn't know that one. Hey, can I have some vines to tie it up with? Think that would work?"

"My love, I would do anything for you, but I will not do that."

I burst out laughing, and the befuddlement on his face grows. "Sorry," I gasp out, the leaves shaking in my grip. "It was just funny for a minute. I'm fine."

"I was going to offer you the lace from my pants," Kanuz says.

"But you need your pants. A vine will work fine."

"The lace would work better."

I poke his pouty lower lip, and he catches my finger gently between his teeth.

"Vines," I tell him. "You keep your pants on. We don't need my favorite toy getting hurt."

He puffs up his chest with pride, releasing my finger and pressing a kiss to the back of my hand instead. "If that is what my glowing flower wants, then that is what she shall get."

"How gallant." I flip my hair, then turn the leaf around, trying to figure out the best way to get max coverage. The foliage is thick and supple, and doesn't tear easily like I thought it might. Kanuz yanks a thick, ropey vine from the wall, sending dirt and grit flying.

"This might work," he says grudgingly, handing me a length of it.

"Fashion, fashion, fashion, baby," I chant. "Make it work! Can you cut a hole in the middle of this?"

Kanuz gives me another bewildered look, then does as I ask, ripping a small hole in the middle of the leaf with his talon.

I clap my hands. "Perfect." I thrust my head through the hole in the leaf's center, and the edges of it barely cover my butt, but it's a hell of a lot better than nothing.

"Vine," I order, and he hands it to me. I tie it around my waist, securing my leaf mini-dress.

Feeling fierce, or maybe manic, who could say, I strut to the base of the tree and back. "And the star of fashion week, Genevieve Durand, modeling her latest." I do a sharp pivot turn, my hands on my hips. The end of my vine belt slaps me in the face.

I cough and bat it down.

"It's *interactive*," I say to Kanuz, who stares at me, open-mouthed. "Couture. Avant-garde."

"Does that mean you are pleased with it?"

"Very much," I tell him, and he smiles as though I've given him everything he ever wanted.

"Are you ready to leave?"

"Fuck yes," I say. "Let's get the hell out of Dodge."

"Dodge?"

"Just go with it."

"Going with it," he agrees, holding out a hand. I lace my fingers in his and follow him into the dark tunnel.

Well, it would be dark, if it weren't for the glow I'm emitting, like some kind of human lightning bug.

CHAPTER
NINETEEN

KANUZ

I CANNOT SEEM to take my eyes from Gen. She glitters in the dark, narrow tunnel, tiny sparks surrounding where she walks. I have to crouch to fit, the space to narrow to stand upright in. But my Gen saunters through like a queen, outfitted in leafy green.

She was beautiful before, but now? Now she is stunning. Her golden hair glows, and the greenish tint to her aura has faded to a mellow sunshine yellow.

"What?" she asks, her face scrunched with concern. "You're looking at me weird."

I shake my head. "I am looking at you because I am in awe of you."

"Don't be. I'm just trying to survive, same as you. I just got the magic water first." Her tone is nervous, different than I've heard her before, and I narrow my eyes.

"Are you worried about the Crigomar?"

"Who wouldn't be nervous about a pair of rabid red and black T-Rexes?"

"In the south, they train them. As pets and a defense mechanism."

She gawks up at me, and I tug her hand, urging her to keep moving through the tunnel.

"They train the dinosaurs?"

"Crigomar."

"Huh. That's kind of amazing."

"I think there is much you will find amazing about our people."

"I think you're right." The words are soft and contemplative, and it tugs at my heart to hear her say it. "How do they train them?"

I pause, unsure, then continue leading her through the tunnel. "I do not know."

I should know. I am the prince of this planet, am I not? But I have neglected our southern brethren. Shame fills me. I should have worked harder to unite our people before now. Instead, I listened to the words of my ill and heartsick father. I mourned the loss of my mother by throwing myself into battle with the Roth, and then soothed the pain of war by throwing myself into bed with any willing female.

"I have not been a good leader," I tell her, my throat closing up.

"What? Why do you say that?" Her steps falter, and my hand goes to her hip, keeping her upright.

"I fear it is my fault that the southern Suevans are restless."

"I thought they were just against us humans." Her breath comes in soft pants, and I slow my pace slightly. She is not as healthy as she was just two weeks ago. That is my fault, too. "Not you in particular."

"I'm the prince. If they are against us, they are against me. I have not been as attentive as I should have been to their problems. Now they find an excuse to use against us."

"Well." There's a sly note to her voice, and when I glance back, she's smirking up at me. "We'll just have to show them the goddess-blessed, right?"

I stop and pull her muscled body into mine, planting a kiss on her glittering lips. "Yes, my love. We will."

But we shouldn't have had to. I shouldn't have had to put my mate through the trials of the many-faced-goddess because of my own shortcomings as the leader of Sueva.

My father was right about me, and as much as that stings to acknowledge, at least now I can grow from the realization.

He was wrong about one thing, though.

I can change, and I will be the king the Suevans deserve.

And I'll have my glittering, golden mate beside me.

Finally, the light appears at the end of the tunnel.

"That better be daylight," Gen says, grumpy again. "I don't think I can take it if it's not."

I blink at her, confused all over again. "What else would it be?"

"Never mind. It was a stupid joke."

"I do not think you are capable of saying anything stupid."

When I glance at her, I expect to see that same smile on her face. I frown when it's not there. Instead, her expression is pinched, concern writ across her face.

"I hope I don't prove you wrong."

The tunnel narrows, the opening overhead half-concealed by vegetation. A root the size of my thigh drapes across the middle of the entrance.

"I will go first, and then I will pull you up behind me," I tell her.

"Works for me."

My talons latch onto the root, and I heave myself up, the walls of the opening clawing at my hide. It's a tight squeeze, but I manage to push myself through, then lie on the ground, extending my arm to Gen.

"Do you trust me, my flower? Take my hand."

"And you'll show me a whole new world?"

"If that is what you wish."

She snorts a laugh, fitting her small hand around my wrist. I clasp hers, and haul her up the opening easily. She fits through easily, sneezing as dust and dirt tumbles into her face.

"We did it," she says, rolling on top of me. "You did it, Kanuz."

She crawls up my chest, her leaf dress riding up to her waist as she wriggles. Her eyes search mine for a long moment, and then her mouth is on mine, her addictive taste pervading my senses.

"Gen," I groan, my hands sliding up her thighs, her waist.

"Don't tear my leaves!" she squeals, then carefully unties the vine belt, tugging her zitsu dress overhead. It flops to the forest floor, and she scooches it away with her toe, her muscles flexing along her thighs. I pull my pants off, too, much faster than before, thank the goddess, and they join her leafy creation.

"I will strive to not damage your new garment," I tell her with a laugh, my hands squeezing her ample ass. "But when we return to my city, I will buy you clothes simply so I can tear them from you."

She arches one eyebrow, pursing her lips. "That sounds wasteful."

"I do not fucking care," I growl, then tug her head back to mine, claiming her mouth for myself. She returns the kiss with fervor, reaching behind her to circle her hand around my hard shaft. I groan as she pumps her fist up and down, all coherent thoughts leaving my head at the pleasure of her touch.

"You are so fucking soft," I tell her, half-sitting up, snagging her pink nipple into my mouth.

She makes a small sound of surprise and pleasure, her hand stilling on my cock before she continues stroking it up and down. My xof begins vibrating, and I growl with the force of my need. Gen's pupils are blown, dark and wide with lust, and her scent tantalizes me.

"Need you," I grit out.

"Then take it," she says, her eyes flashing with challenge.

"Fuck," I manage, my hands going to her waist, lifting her off where she straddles my chest and flipping her to her stomach, forcing her to her hands and knees.

She gives a soft moan. Her cunt drips with her need, and I press my hand gently in between her shoulders, forcing her ass higher in the air.

"Look at you, splayed open for me." I nudge her knees wider apart, and she looks back at me, her eyes wild and glassy. "Glowing and wet, the way I want you to be, always."

Bending down, I lap at her entrance, savoring her taste, her warmth.

"Kanuz," she says, her legs shaking.

"Tell me," I command, and when she reaches back to touch me, I circle her wrist with my fingers, pressing it firmly behind her back. I lick her again, and she cries out.

Still, I wait. Precum drips from the tip of my cock, and I ache with the need to fill her.

"I want you, my prince," she says, her voice low and needy.

I lick her again, rewarding her. She shudders, and I keep one hand on her wrist at her back, the other on her hips, keeping her still. She undulates against my mouth, her movements frantic.

I let out a harsh laugh, then give into my own need, slamming into her. I release her wrist, and she immediately braces herself against the ground, pushing herself harder against me.

"So demanding. So perfect," I tell her. Slowly, I run one talon down the delicate line of her spine, and she shivers in response. I pull out, savoring the way she clenches around me.

When I slam back into her, she lets out a low cry. My teeth clench together, and my xof vibrates so hard the round curve of her ass shakes with it. The sight undoes what little control I have left, and I pick up the pace, matching her frenzied rhythm.

"Kanuz," she breathes, and I have never heard such a perfect sound as my name on her lips while my cock slides in and out of my wife. "I love you."

"My flower, my Gen," I groan, my cock throbbing as I spill my seed deep inside her. "I love you, too."

I snake an arm around her waist, pulling her up so that her back is flush with my chest. My cock pulses inside her, and I lick my fingers, then push my hand between her spread legs, working the small nub of her pleasure as I rock back and forth.

Her head falls back against my chest, her eyes closed in pleasure. I stroke her, watching the quick succession of expressions that flit across her face, raising my other hand to palm her breast.

"Kanuz," she moans, and then she's clenching around my cock, rippling and pulsing as her wetness soaks my thighs.

"I love you," I tell her again, kissing against the delicate plane of her collar, the dip below her neck. "Now, my love, I think we are ready to continue to Edrobaz."

"It's going to take us a year, at this rate."

"If it is a year spent like this, I am not sure I can complain." I kiss her neck, sweaty from the pleasure I wrung from her, salty and sweet just like the woman herself.

She slides off my cock, turning to press her body against mine. Her arms wrap around my neck, her chest heaving as we hold each other. "Then I guess it's a good thing we have a lifetime together."

Warmth spreads through me at her words, and I kiss the top of her golden head, squeezing her to me. She lets out a tiny squeal, making me chuckle.

"Come, wife. Put your zitsu leaf back on. We are starting our journey home."

She stands slowly, stretching with a smile on her face, and I marvel at her, at the glow on her skin, the sated, happy look on her face.

My wife.

GEN

HIKING around in the Suevan jungle without boots sucks. Even with poor Kanuz carrying me most of the way, it's less than fun. Not to mention, my new glow attracts every bloodthirsty insect for miles. I scratch at a bump on my shoulder, hungry and tired.

That's when we hear them.

The unmistakable sound of the hellish T-Rexes, screaming to each other. Under my bare feet, the ground shakes.

"I did not just survive my very own temple of doom to be eaten by a dinosaur," I say through gritted teeth.

Kanuz says nothing, simply grabs me where I stand, throwing me over one shoulder and taking off at a sprint. How he still has the energy, I do not know.

"The Crigomar will not eat you while I live, my flower."

Considering they're chasing both of us, it's not very reassuring, but I stay quiet and do my best sack of potatoes impression. Mmm. Potatoes. What I wouldn't give for a giant baked potato slathered in butter and cheese. Or fries. Salty, greasy cheese fries with bacon and sour cream and little slivers of green onions.

The terrifying cacophony from the giant reptiles gets closer, and real fear grips me. I don't think our odds of a giant swamp snake appearing to save us are very high, considering we're on dry land.

As my worry grows, my glow intensifies. I stare down at my hands, annoyed. Kanuz's pace eats up the ground, ignoring the underbrush where it slaps against his thick hide.

My heart skips a beat. The noise of the giant dinosaurs dies, and it's like the entire jungle *breathes*.

The tree cover ends suddenly, giving way to a roiling pool of water. A waterfall crashes into the expanse of blue. White froth bubbles and foams, the white noise nearly canceling out the sound of the raging beasts on our tail.

I swallow. After surviving the tentacle monster in the temple, I'm never looking at a lake the same way ever again.

And with the sound of the waterfall, there's no way we'll hear the Crigomar until they're right on us.

"Fuck," Kanuz says, and I can just barely hear the word. He sets me down, and annoyance steals over me as I pat my thighs for a weapon I don't have.

Nope, all I have is my dress made of leaves and newly glowing skin.

I look like Peter Pan's fairy sidekick, if Peter Pan were a scaled lizard man who likes to fuck.

Kanuz pushes me behind him, and I sigh in annoyance. Sure, rationally it makes sense that he would protect me, and as much as I've enjoyed rediscovering my touchy-feely side, I miss being able to protect myself.

Sure enough, a red and black head bursts through the foliage, and I tense, glancing behind me at the crashing waterfall. Would they follow me in? Would I be a wet tasty morsel instead of a dry one? Maybe they'd prefer that, like a cat I had growing up refused to eat anything but canned wet food, the diva.

Or would the current from the waterfall bash me to smithereens against the sharp rocks jutting into the water?

So many fun options on this planet.

The second Crigomar appears, and Kanuz spreads his arms out wide, like he's chasing a pet dog back from something.

Adrenaline and lack of food must be making me punchy, because I laugh.

"What?" he asks, yelling over the sound of the water.

"I just… Do you think that's going to work?"

He shoots me an injured look, then immediately goes taut.

Two Suevans appear from the edge of the jungle, their energy rifles at their sides. One has an energy knife slung across his hip, and my fingers itch to take it.

The weirdest thing though? They don't look worried about the Crigomar. I straighten in surprise. One of the Suevans pats the nearest Crigomar's stomach, and the dinosaur whuffs. Whuffs! Like a damn horse.

"What the fuck?"

The other Suevan points at me, and I can't hear what they're saying over the water, and I sure as shit can't read Suevan lips.

They holster their weapons, smiling broadly at us.

"Who are they?" I ask Kanuz, caught between relief and the worry this is a *trap*.

"Southerners."

I squint at them, the waterfall misting my back making me shiver. "How can you tell?"

"They have redder abdomens… and they are controlling the Crigomar."

"Really?" I can't see any difference, but whatever. "Wait. Doesn't that mean they're hunting us?"

One beckons, the other raising a fist. Kanuz returns the gesture, and I realize it must be some kind of greeting. They point at me again, their faces full of wonder.

Oh, yeah. My newfound bioluminescence.

"I guess we're about to find out if you were right about the temple treasure," I say.

Kanuz shoots me a dark look, worry clear on his face. He

slings an arm around my shoulders, and we walk together towards the newcomers—and the Crigomar.

A rope of saliva stretches from one of the dinosaur's sharp teeth, and its diamond pupils contract as I get closer. It makes an odd keening noise, and I recoil instinctively.

"No wonder they have been impossible to control today," the nearest alien says. Kanuz's fingers flex, talons outstretched. "Look at her."

"What happened to you, little human female?" the second alien says, not unkindly.

They're both staring at me with open fascination, and I glare at them. "Well, for one, your dinosaurs want to eat me."

Kanuz makes a startled noise.

The nearest alien looses a laugh, and the other one bites his cheeks as though he's trying not to.

"The Crigomar are not going to eat you."

Kanuz seems as surprised as I am by that news.

"Oh, really? Is that why they tried to eat us only…" I falter, unsure of how much time has passed since we fled into the temple ruins. "A few days ago they did!"

"No, they did not. And that explains why we could not find them." He exchanges a weary glance with the other Suevan, who still seems on the verge of laughter.

"Find us?" Kanuz says, and there's none of the easygoing male that's been quick to laugh with me the last few weeks. No. This Kanuz drips condescension and command, every inch of his body transformed into someone I hardly recognize.

This is Kanuz, Prince of Sueva. I blink. I like this Kanuz, too.

"What do you mean, find us? Do you know who I am? Do you see her? Do you know what that light means?"

"Of course we know who you are, Prince. We may be working together with Warlord Draz, but we are not going to bow and scrape to you. And as far as the princess, that light means she ingested a large amount of Nidoth. Enough that she'll likely glow for years."

"I give it seven to ten," the other Suevan adds, a speculative look on his face. "Did she bathe in it?"

I bark a laugh. "Nidoth?"

"Yes, pretty human, Nidoth. It's what we use to help train our Crigomar." His green taloned hand stands out on the black and red hide of the dinosaur. "It's a light trigger. They respond to it like lures. Only thing that works when they're freshly hatched. It's an ancient formula we have kept secret, passed down by the handmaidens of the many-faced-goddess herself. We make it in small batches, as it is time intensive and hard to find the ingredients. The only real function for it is training the Crigomar to respond to commands when they are young."

"That's why they've been chasing you. Once they get old enough, they don't need it anymore, but with you radiating it like that..." He scratches his chin. "I am relieved to know that it was not a sign they had slipped our control completely."

The Crigomar whuffs in response, and I stare up at the big animal, whose gaze is still fixed on me. Kanuz's arm slips lower, around my waist, his fingers just under my breast. It's possessive, and he juts his chin out aggressively at the southern Suevans.

"So you do not recognize this as a symbol of the goddess? Her glowing skin?" There's a faint hint of confusion and disappointment in his voice. "Is this not a sign that human females are meant to be here?"

Both males shuffle, distinctly uncomfortable. "About that. After we met a human female, we are not so opposed to them any longer."

I blow out a huge breath, sagging against Kanuz. That's a damn relief to hear. So glad I'm not going to be fed to a dino, after all. Surviving Jurassic Park, one alien at a time, that's me.

"But her glowing skin... the gift of the goddess—" He breaks off. He doesn't say it, but I know what he's thinking. All that fucking work... and for what?

The Southern Suevans were already convinced to join our side.

"The glowing skin is lovely, to be sure, Princess. We mean no disrespect." They glance at me nervously, then away, like they're afraid Kanuz might smack them around if they look at my Tinker-bell-sparkling-self too long. "Useful, if you knew how to train a Crigomar."

"Honestly," I take a deep breath, pausing, "I'm relieved."

Kanuz stares at me, something like shock on his face. "It is my turn to apologize, my flower. I did not consider how you felt about this."

"Hey." I shrug, grinning at him. "It all turned out for the best. Now I don't have to do anything but glow, no pressure at all."

He bows his head. "I should not have made you feel pressured in the first place."

"Kanuz," I say, then pull his head to mine, touching our fore-heads together. "It's okay. I'm relieved, but I would have done it. If it would have helped, I would have done it."

"I am truly the luckiest male, to have a wife such as you."

"I won't argue there," I say, winking, and start to lean forward, wanting to kiss him, wanting to—

"Warlord Draz is sending for more human females for us," one of the Southern Suevan interrupts. "He will be thrilled to know you are both safe, as will his Ni-Kee."

"Ni-Kee… Niki?! You've seen Niki?" My throat closes up, emotion choking me. Kanuz squeezes my shoulder. "Is she okay? Is everyone okay?" I step closer, out of Kanuz's grip. The Crigomar nearest me lowers his head, and hot breath cascades over my head. Saliva drips onto my shoulder, and the beast nudges me gently with a giant nose.

Caught between horror and fascination, I stare up at it, momentarily forgetting my question. Hard to focus with a red T-Rex acting like a dog who wants to be petted. I scratch under its chin, and it makes the strangest sound, somewhere between a purr and a low whine.

"That one is only going to respond to her now," the alien says forlornly. "You'll have to take it as a mating gift, Prince."

"Your Ni-Kee is fierce and beautiful," the first Suevan

responds finally, longing clear in his face. "As are you. She does not glow, however. She disarmed several of our men. And the Roth."

"That's right, she is clever and a master strategist. She single-handedly brought him down."

"We helped."

They both nod, and I stare at them with wide eyes. I'm so fucking relieved to hear Niki made it out unscathed, it takes me a moment to register the other bomb they've dropped.

"A Roth?" I finally manage.

"What do you mean, a Roth?" Kanuz growls at the same time.

The dinosaur nudges my forehead again, and I resume scratching it, only slightly terrified of what happens when I stop.

"Is he alive?" I ask. "Or did Niki kill him?"

The dinosaur makes a soft roaring sound, and I try not to jump.

"It knows you're upset," the Suevan says, scowling at me like it was my choice to take his dinosaur from him. "And no, she did not kill him, though she did maim him. It was a stunning sight to see. However, in her brilliance, she decided it best to leave him alive for questioning."

"I will rip his spine out and gift it to you, my flower," Kanuz tells me.

My lips twist to the side. "Ah, that won't be necessary. But thanks. That's really thoughtful of you."

"Say the word, and—" He closes his fist and makes a yanking motion. "No more Roth."

"Uh, if Niki thought he had information we needed, then I think we should save the spine-ripping for later, don't you?"

"Later," he agrees. The dino whuffs again, sending more slobber down my leaf. "Why are the Roth here?" Kanuz asks.

"The same reason the females are here for us. The virus hit their people, too. They seek a cure. Or they did. Now? They seek human females."

My jaw drops open.

I turn to Kanuz. "When will the tech shipment get to Earth?"

"It is already on its way, my flower," he says gently, but I know him well enough now to tell he's troubled, too. That he's thinking what I'm thinking.

If Roth wants human females to procreate with, Earth is in big trouble.

"We need to get back to my crew."

"Take us to Edrobaz," Kanuz says at the same time.

"I hope the newest shipment of human females has many just like you and Ni-Kee," one of the southern Suevans sighs.

A wet, rasping tongue licks across my ear, and I shove the dinosaur's head away in disgust. "Stop it, Steve."

"Steeeve?" one of the aliens repeats. "What a strange, foreign name."

"Very formidable," the other adds. "Wise choice, Princess."

Steve lowers his head again, butting my chest so hard I nearly fall on my ass. "We don't have time to lose, my dudes. Let's go."

It's not a great princess impression. I don't have the same panache as Kanuz does, but the other Suevans stare at me, something like awe on their faces.

"She called us *her* dudes," one whispers.

"Is this a high rank amongst your people?"

I glance sidelong at Kanuz, trying to figure out how I should play it.

This is just too fucking weird. I nod my head, pursing my lips. "Absolutely. From now on, you're my dudes."

They both drop to one knee, fists held up.

Right.

What problems could possibly come from this?

Kanuz grins at me, that too-hot-for-his-own-good smirk back in place.

"To Edrobaz!" I yell, losing my head completely.

They don't cheer or repeat me though, unfortunately for my delusions of grandeur. They just get up, nod at me, and set off through the jungle.

"Did that play out like you wanted it to?" Kanuz asks, sly amusement in his voice.

"Not exactly, but it sure as shit could have gone worse."

All in all, I'm not mad about it. My limbs are intact. I have a dinosaur friend I've dubbed Steve, and I've added two former separatists to my troupe of dudes, which now totals… two.

I don't know what having them as my dudes means yet, but I'll figure it out. Probably.

CHAPTER
TWENTY-ONE

KANUZ

THE SEPARATISTS DID NOT NEED me to unite them. They did not even need the symbol of the goddess' blessing that Gen wears on her skin, the one we risked life and limb to get, to see reason.

All they needed was to have hope for their future.

As we all do.

I mull it over as Edrobaz nears in the distance. The atmospheric bubble shimmers slightly in the mountain air, crisp and clean, but too cold for my Gen, who shivers constantly. We made it here much faster than I would have imagined. The temple courtyard tunnel dumped us further north in the jungle than I'd realized.

"I am grateful you found us," I tell the southern Suevans.

"We are glad to have had the opportunity to come to know you better."

"Especially since we are now the princess' dudes."

Gen shoots me a nervous look, and I bite back a laugh at the consternated expression on her face. She was so eager to include these two and make them feel welcome, that she did not quite think through the ramifications of giving them the title of dude.

I hate to think what they will do when they find out she says it to everyone.

Gen's already won them over, though. How could she not? She's funny and brave, and has not complained once, despite her teeth clattering together.

The zitsu leaf is an ill-choice for clothing, and the southerners gave her a blanket from their packs, but it's still not enough for her fragile human skin.

Gen's eyes go wide as she takes in the city sprawled before us. Early evening mist clings to the primeval trees bursting from the mountaintop city, the myza that the dwellers here make their homes in. A wall surrounds the city proper, and as we approach, the dirt trail gives way to polished stone.

"This is really… I've never seen trees that big before."

"I think you will like my city, too."

"The southern cities are likewise beautiful, Princess," a Southerner butts in, gazing at Gen with blatant adoration that sets my teeth on edge. "You should visit them soon. I know the few of our people that remain there would like to see you for themselves. To see what it is we're fighting for."

Gen's throat bobs, and then she inclines her head nobly. "That sounds like a great idea."

The southerners beam.

Behind us, the Crigomar let up a resounding roar, angry at the barrier that keeps them away from the city proper.

"Knock it off, Steve!" Gen bellows, so loud that the southerners wince. The roaring dies, replaced by a plaintive whine.

"I never thought I'd be telling a dinosaur to shut up."

The great gate of Edrobaz begins to grind open, and we all swing our attention to it.

"Oh my god!" a female voice shrieks. "Gen is alive! And she's radioactive!" A dark-haired curvaceous beauty bounces out of the gate, sprinting for where I hold Gen in my arms, after her poor feet couldn't handle the rough terrain any longer.

"Radioactive? Officer Durand, have you been handling unsanctioned materials?" This voice is strong and laced with humor, and another human woman saunters from the doorway, draped in traditional Suevan fabric. The woman's face contorts as she takes Gen in, and then she, too, is running towards us. I clutch her tighter to my chest, feeling possessive and violent.

"Ni-Kee!" one of the southerners says, his delight in seeing the human evident.

"Gen, what the fuck?" the brunette says. "Are you okay? Why do you look like Tinkerbell on an acid trip?"

"Hey, Bex." Gen's voice is faint, and her body tenses. She inhales deeply, and I know she's trying to contain her soft heart, trying to stay strong as she always does. "It's damn good to see you."

"Likewise." Bex glances up at me, her lips pursing. "I guess you know by now the dude who's carrying you is your husband, yeah?"

"Dude?" One of the aliens asks.

"He is a dude, too?" the other adds.

"Why don't you two go ahead inside and ah…" Gen trails off, clearly flummoxed.

"Obtain some rest and food for your service. On the prince," I finish for her. They nod once, then all but race inside Edrobaz. She squeezes my arm in gratitude, and I keep walking, Ni-Kee and Bex keeping pace beside us.

"Are you hurt?" Ni-Kee asks her, shooting me a careful look. Like she does not trust that I haven't been the one to hurt her. Anger rises inside me, uncoiling like a venomous snake. "Did you hurt him?"

Gen laughs. "I'm hungry, I'm cold, and I'm tired, but I'm not hurt. And I didn't hurt him. Much." She raises one eyebrow, and Bex sighs, glancing between us.

The Crigomar starts up another plaintive roar.

"SO HELP ME, STEVE," Gen thunders, and the roar cuts off quickly.

Bex's eyebrows shoot up. "Uh. Did you just yell at a dinosaur?"

"She is goddess-blessed," I explain. Bex's brow furrows, and I realize with a sudden shock that she cannot understand me. I am going to have a long talk with my scientists at Perzivor.

"Riiiiight," Ni-Kee says. "Prince Kanuz, it's a pleasure to meet you, by the way. We've all been worried sick about you both. It sounds like you've got one hell of a story to tell. I'm Captain Jacks. This is Bex." She nods at the brunette. "We'd like to help Gen adjust to life here, if you don't mind leaving her with us."

"She goes nowhere without me," I hiss, snapping my jaws at her.

A familiar figure stands at the gate, a vicious energy sword strapped to his back.

"Prince," Draz intones, dipping his chin in greeting, one fist raised toward me.

"First Warlord."

"I would appreciate it if you stopped threatening my mate."

"I would appreciate it if she stopped trying to take *my* mate from me." No one will take her from me. My golden flower is mine *alone*.

"No one is taking me from you, Kanuz, calm your tits."

Bewildered, I stare down at my precious mate. "I do not have tits. Even if I did, I do not know how I would calm them."

Ni-Kee snorts, and Gen gives her a beleaguered look. "Here's the thing, Kanuz, we've been in the jungle for—" She wrinkles her nose.

"Sixteen and a half days," Bex supplies.

"Thank you, Officer Abbas. I can tell you right now that my crew wants to debrief, make sure I'm healthy, and I want to do the same with them."

"But I want—"

"I appreciate that you may not have planned on this, but *this* is what is going to happen." Her voice is icey calm, and I blink at her, loving it. My cock gets hard. I haven't heard this tone from her before.

I grin at her, my cock aching. Her eyes narrow, a smile playing about her lips, and I know she can feel where my hardness nudges against her.

She raises her shimmering hand to my cheek, pulling me down to kiss my cheek.

"Let me touch base with my crew, Kanuz," she whispers. "You go get intel on the Roth, check in with your warlords, and then we can reconvene and make a plan for how to protect Earth, if they haven't already. And then..." She trails off, her small, smooth tongue licking across my cheekbone.

"And then I will ravage you, again and again."

"I can't speak Suevan, but I think I know what he just said." Bex groans, pinching the bridge of her nose. "They're just as insufferable as you and Draz."

Ni-Kee rolls her eyes, but there's a hint of a smile on her face. "Can you walk, Gen, or do you need him to carry you? We'll get you cleaned up and clean clothes and some food, and we'll debrief while we take care of you."

Gen taps on my shoulder, and I let her down. "I can walk. I just left my boots behind." She tugs the blanket around her shoulders.

"You really do look radioactive," Ni-Kee says speculatively.

"I'll tell Carmen and Tati to run some tests," Bex says. "Do you feel sick?"

"I'm not radioactive."

"She is *healthy*," I snarl. "She was blessed by the goddess."

"Easy," Draz murmurs, his eyebrows raised.

Gen slips from my grasp, giving my hand a final squeeze, and then she disappears through the gate, flanked by her crew members.

My hands fist at my sides, clenched so tight my talons bite into my hide. I stare after her long after her shimmer has disappeared into the fading light, Draz watching me with careful eyes.

"She is safe," he finally says, his tone ripe with understanding. "My mate feels a solemn duty to her crew. Is it true you received the blessing of the goddess?"

"Gen did." My throat closes up, and I fight the need to chase after her. I do not want her out of my sight. I want her in my arms. I want her back, and I want it now.

"How?"

I sigh, and Draz closes the gate on the jungle behind us as we begin to walk through his city. "Take me to the Roth, and I will tell you. I long to make jewelry from his bones, but I wish to know what his race has in store for Earth."

Draz is silent for a long moment, then nods once. "You have changed. She has changed you."

"She is *everything*," I tell him vehemently.

And I will keep the vow I made to myself to protect her, and her people.

I will get the information we need from the Roth, one way or another.

CHAPTER
TWENTY-TWO

GEN

THE TREE HOUSES are just as fucking cool on the inside as they seemed on the outside. "This is your house?" I ask Niki, awed by the sight. Everything just... works. Flows together. Natural wood walls of the hollow trees—the myza—mesh with soft furniture and plush rugs.

"Yeah, but you're welcome to bunk with the rest of the crew if you feel safer there than with the Prince."

I snort, sure she's joking.

She doesn't laugh, and neither does Bex.

"Why are you both staring at me like that? I expect the third degree from the captain, but not you, Chaos Queen," I tell Bex.

"Prince Kanuz has a reputation," Niki says slowly. "Are you sure you are all right?"

"What, you think he Stockholm Syndromed me into falling in love with him? Not a chance. As if I would allow that to happen."

Carmen looks up from where she's drawing my blood, using a ridiculously advanced device that must be Suevan, because I can't make heads or tails of it. She knows what the fuck she's doing though, thank God. "Durand, you can't will your way out of

Stockholm Syndrome. You've been alone in what sounds to be a desperate situation for weeks now. We're doing our due diligence to ensure that you're safe."

"Thanks," I tell her acidly, yanking my arm away. "What, so you can believe that Captain Jacks is happily fucking her alien boy toy, but Durand is so bitchy that she must have had a lobotomy to fall in love?"

"You really are in love," Bex says, her voice moony and eyes huge. "I want to hear all about it. All the dirty details."

"Why can't you understand them yet?" I ask, dodging her question. I don't feel like being interrogated about my sex life. My excellent, really great, phenomenal alien sex life.

"We can't figure out why some of us understand them and some don't. Carmen, Tati and I have been working on it, but so far, it's speculation. They're symbiont tech. Cutting edge, even for the Suevans. We think there must be some kind of neural path rearrangement that they facilitate, but it might take longer on some than others. Tell me about Kanuz. He has quite the reputation among the Suevans. Has he forced you?"

"What?" I ask, aghast. "No. He's been more gentlemanly than any guy I ever dated on Earth."

"You didn't exactly hang around with the cream of the crop," Bex says.

"Your pulse just spiked," Carmen observes. She winks at me, and I glare back at her.

"What do you mean Kanuz has a reputation?"

"The other Suevans, they just say he gets around."

"So what, he's a manwhore?" I shrug one shoulder. "He's married now. To me. I'm not worried."

Niki's eyes narrow like she's going to say something else. Instead, she shakes her head, digging through a pile of clothes and tossing a pair of slippers into a basket, then adds several colorful swathes of fabric to it.

"Touchy, touchy," Bex says.

"You would be touchy, too, if the first thing your friends want to do when they see you after you've spent fifteen—"

"Sixteen and a half," Bex supplies unhelpfully.

"Sixteen and a half days in the alien jungle, fighting for your life against giant snakes and having crazy dinosaurs falling in love with you and making your way through an ancient temple full of death traps and tentacle monsters, and then you get to safety, your friends want to bitch about how your husband was a man whore before you were sold to him in marriage *by your own fucking government!*" I'm yelling now, nearly shaking with the residual adrenaline of everything I've been through. I hate that I can't get control of myself. I hate that I've slipped right back into the old, asshole version of myself, and I sit there steaming, staring at them and daring them to say something else.

"Blood work's clean," Carmen announces, staring down at the machine with an awkward expression. "You're dehydrated and your white blood cell count is unusually high, but not so high that it's triggering any alarms. I recommend rest, water, food, and more rest." She wrinkles her nose. "And a bath. With soap. No jungle adventures for at least fourteen days."

"Hey, that's in time for the warlord trials," Bex says.

I don't know what that is, but I'm too distracted by Niki to ask.

She exhales, relief clear on her face. She obviously thought something was wrong with me, and it hurts my feelings. It hurts my feelings that the only me even my best friend knows is one that's mean and bitchy and trigger happy.

That she thought seeing me smiling and relaxed in Kanuz's arms was a sure sign something was wrong.

And I can't even be fucking mad at her about it because it's my own stupid fault. I'm the one who's been unremittingly mean. I'm the one who only ever let everyone see the wall I put around myself, even my closest friends and crew.

"I'm sorry," I say quietly.

Niki's expression tightens, and Bex's mouth opens wide in astonishment.

"I'm sorry I yelled at you. You don't deserve that." I rub a hand across the back of my neck. I blow out a breath, making myself meet their eyes in turn. "I have been a shitty friend. None of you deserve the way I treat you." I lapse into silence, exhaustion stealing over me.

Carmen blinks owlishly up at me, checking the machine again. "Maybe I start you on an antibiotic course just in case. Some supplements. Maybe a banana bag. They have something here that works even better than what we use at home."

"Sure," I say, too tired to fight.

I look up at Niki, and she's biting her lip, the way she does right before she lunges straight for her candy stash when she's stressed.

"I care about Kanuz. I love him. What we went through out there, it was… life-changing. It changed me." I swallow down the lump forming in my throat. "*He* changed me. He reminded me that I don't have to be so fucking hard all the time. He reminded me that true strength means being weak and asking for help sometimes, too. So thank you, thank you for looking out for me. I know you mean well, and I love you for it. I'm going to get cleaned up now."

"Gen," Niki says, her face softening. "I'm so glad you're back."

I yelp as something stings my wrist, searing up my veins, and Carmen winces. "Sorry. That's the antibiotic and supplement cocktail. If anything nasty's floating around in your bloodstream, it'll be gone in a jiff."

"Cool," I say, the pain already fading.

"The clothes in the basket should fit you."

"Oh, am I going to look like I belong in *I Dream Of Jeannie* like the rest of you?"

"They're comfy," Bex says, plucking at her voluminous purple sleeve. "And pretty."

"They are pretty," I admit.

Niki's eyes spark. "I have makeup."

"I don't remember the last time I put on makeup."

"I'll do yours while we fully debrief. Get cleaned up, I'll order food in, and we'll look at the makeup Bex made and catch everyone up on everything."

"Sounds official."

"Fuck official," Captain Jacks says. "Fuck the Federation, and fuck everything but getting that tech safely to Earth."

"And fuck the Roth," I add for good measure. "Sounds like a plan. I'll be back when I don't stink."

"And literally fuck the Suevans," Bex adds.

We all stare at her for a second before Niki breaks the tension by laughing. I shake my head. "Where's the bathroom?"

Niki points to a door in the back of the room, and I stand up, heading for it.

"Wait," Bex says plaintively, and from the shit-eating-grin on her face, I'm already worried about what's going to come out of her mouth. "Tell me more about this tentacle monster." Her eyes are huge, and she bats her lashes.

Shaking my head, I laugh as I leave them for the siren call of hygiene.

CHAPTER
TWENTY-THREE

KANUZ

THE MERE SIGHT of the Roth's gray, swirl-patterned skin makes me see red.

"Come to try your hand with me, Prince?" he asks, malice clear in his gaze. "I've always found royalty too soft to do what needs to be done."

I snarl, smashing my hand against the wall of the cell.

Dergoz's talons prick my hide as he pulls me away. "You are in no condition to interrogate him."

"He means to harvest human females from Earth. He does not deserve to share the air we breathe."

"You are well and truly in a mating frenzy, are you not, Prince?" Alvez asks. "We have sent another convoy to protect the shipment. There is nothing he can do from here to hurt your mate, or any other human."

"Then he is of no use to us," I growl, narrowing my eyes at the foul alien in the cage. He's built similarly to Suevans, big of build, muscle packed on, but that's where the similarities end. Though quick-healing, the Roth have velvet-like skin closer to the human texture than our tough hides.

"Wait," the Roth calls out, and something sparks behind him.

"Did you scan him?" I ask, concern building at the small lights appearing at his shoulder.

"Of course we scanned him," Draz growls. "We followed every protocol and then some."

"I mean no offense, First Warlord." I try to keep my voice even, but the words still snap with impatience.

"Wait," the Roth repeats, and his voice is desperate, the tone unlike anything I've ever heard from his species. "I have information."

"You would sell your Overlord out for your life?" I ask, wary at his sudden change in tone.

"Not for *my* life." He shakes his head, his strange eyes glittering with an inner fire. He points at his shoulder.

"It's a trick," Alvez snarls.

I am unsure. He seems… sincere. And Alvez is predisposed to believe the worst about the Roth, thanks to his time spent in their fighting pits. Not that the rest of us believe anything good about them, but he has more reason to hate them than anyone.

"This is a tracking beacon," he says. "My brothers implanted it in me after the first wave conscription. You know of this," he growls at Alvez. "I recognize you from the fighting pits. You know we were forced to join the Overlord's cause on pain of death or torture. And yet you are blinded by your madness."

"Enough." I shove Alvez back, his eyes burning with anger. "Kanuz is right. Let us listen to what he says."

"My younger brothers avoided the conscription by being too young to join up. Even the Roth Overlord has limits. Or, he used to. They injected it when I slept, and I left it in."

"He's bluffing," Dergoz declares. "Our tech would have found it."

"It isn't regular tech," the Roth stands, looming in the small cell, pacing back and forth. "It cannot be taken out. They were young and foolish and wanted to know where I was. They keep track of me. And they just activated it, because my ship hasn't sent them an update in seventeen days."

"Your young brothers are on their way here," I repeat slowly. "And you would bargain information in return for sparing their lives."

He nods once, the muscle in his jaw twitching so hard I can tell giving us just that small amount of information irritates him to no end.

"Check the scans," Draz says, and Dergoz moves quickly through the doors. "Advise the techs to stand down, wait and watch protocols."

"This is a bad idea," Alvez says, shaking his head. "The Roth are expert liars."

The gray alien slams his hands against the cell wall. "It is not a lie. I lost everyone. Everyone, to the virus. Except my brothers." His face is tight, and the tips of his hair begin to turn blue, then red… like they're burning.

I tilt my head. In all my battles against his species, I have never seen that.

"I would die gladly for my brothers. I will tell you what you want to know, and then you can be done with me. Just give me proof that they are safe, and I will tell you everything I know about the Overlord and his plans for Sueva and Earth. I'm dead anyway. Once the Overlord knows I've been caught, he would send a team out to finish me off if I ever get off this planet."

"Small Roth freighter headed inbound," Dergoz reports, his voice coming through the datapad in Draz's hand.

"He spoke true," I say, studying the Roth. "What is your name?"

"They call me Nydo." He grits his teeth, as though simply telling us that pains him.

It's a start.

"Tell us everything you can think of, and we will fact-check it with what we already know." It's a dangerous game, to deal with spies and double-crossers, but there's enough on the line that I think it's worth the gamble. Worst case, he doesn't give us anything new, or he tries leading us to an easily found out trap. I have confidence in our ability to see through any deceptions.

Best case, we have a Roth traitor in our holding cells and a new insight into their operations.

Draz catches my eye, nodding his head. He's thinking the same thing.

"We will record our conversation and have our techs fact-checking as you speak. If you lie, your brothers find out exactly how our interplanetary defense tech works. Understood?"

The reddish tinge travels up his hair, over his shoulders.

"What is that?" Draz asks.

The alien slumps against the hard bench on the back wall. "It is a family problem," he says roughly. "A *very* old family problem." He turns to look at us, and his gaze is tired. "What do you want to know?"

Draz rattles off a list of questions, and as pleased as I am that we're making progress with the Roth prisoner, Nydo, I'm distracted.

I want to tell Gen. I want to see Gen. I wish she were here at my side, helping me make decisions.

Holding my hand while doing so.

"So far, everything is true," a voice chirps over Draz's comm tablet.

Nydo watches us with wary eyes, distaste clear on his face. I am shocked he would turn traitor to save his brothers.

I can't help but think that perhaps there is more to the Roth problem than any of us would care to admit.

We spend the next two hours drilling down information from our newly pliant captive, until the cell wall finally turns opaque, signaling the communication barrier is sealed between us.

Draz fixes me with a knowing look.

"You are distracted, Prince."

I run a hand through my hair. "I long for my mate." I purse my lips. "Does it fade? The hunger?"

"It has only been a week or so for us." He laughs, shaking his head. "But no. I cannot imagine it will. As understandably distracted as you are, you did very well with him."

I should not need his praise. I outrank him, as a Prince, even though he's several years older than I and three times as experienced.

"Thank you," I tell Draz seriously. "I want to do the best I can by Sueva. By *all* of Sueva."

"By your glowing female, too, I imagine." His scarred face twitches, and I can tell he's holding in a laugh.

"I will not deny it."

Dergoz, the Brute, makes an irritated noise from behind us. "All you two think about is burying yourselves in their soft cunts. You are both insufferable."

Draz and I both turn to him, furious.

He bows his head immediately. "Apologies."

"You would do well to make amends with your wife, Brute," Draz spits.

"The humans are too soft for our species," Dergoz retorts, and I have a sneaking suspicion this is not the first time they have had this conversation.

"Kanuz and I have not had any problems," Draz returns.

Dergoz snaps his teeth, his tail smashing the wall behind. Stiffly, he dips his head at me, and walks out.

"What happened?"

Draz shrugs. "I do not know. Neither he nor Bex will discuss it."

"Bex? The dark-haired one?"

"Yes." Draz smiles. "She makes my Ni-Kee laugh. It saddens me that the Brute refuses to give her a chance. Especially when Bex is willing and so many are not."

"The females are still unwilling?"

"More or less." He shrugs, looking uncomfortable. "I am disgusted by what their Federation did. It is despicable."

"Agreed." We both fall silent.

"The southerners said you sent word to have more females brought here."

Draz chuckles. "That would be my Ni-Kee's doing. She negotiated their help in turning on the Roth in return for bringing more mates for them. Of course, the women would have to choose to come here." His expression darkens.

"The Roth captured you?" I ask, stunned. For the First Warlord to be caught unawares… That is something I truly thought I would never see. He claps me on the shoulder.

"Come, Kanuz, let us walk and talk. I am eager to return to my mate, though hopefully she will not be too tired from training for the Trials."

"She thinks to compete in the Trials?" Good for her. A human female as a Suevan Warlord. "Perhaps Dergoz would not be so quick to dismiss his wife if Niki succeeds."

"Oh, there is no *if* about it. She will succeed. I have no doubt about it." He shakes his head, his eyes shining with affection for her.

"I am glad you are well pleased with her," I tell him sincerely.

"As am I for you, my friend. I never thought this day would come."

We walk through the long hall together, leaving the Roth to his own devices in his cell.

TWENTY-FOUR

GEN

"I FEEL LIKE A CLOWN."

"Shut up. I barely put any on you." Bex wields the pot of red-tinted balm like a weapon, and I eye her warily. "It's literally cheek stain. It's not like I put falsies on you and airbrushed your skin."

"I'm glowing already," I tell her irritably. "Don't start talking about airbrushing my skin."

"Yeah, honestly, we could bottle whatever the hell it is you drank, sell it on Earth, and make an absolutely killing in the beauty industry."

"You said I look like acid trip Tinkerbell."

"It's a mood. It's a look. It's a lifestyle."

I glare at her, and she dabs something soft on my lips.

"Okay," Niki interrupts from where she's sprawled across something that looks like a sofa, but isn't quite a sofa. "Let me get this straight."

She pauses, tapping on what they call a comm tablet, and looks like a futuristic piece of smokey glass. Elon Musk would shit a brick if he saw it. "You fell through a trap door, solved death trap after death trap, and then decided to drink this biolu-minescent liquid, and Kanuz thinks it's the treasure of their goddess?"

"It looked. Like. Water." I grit out. "It tasted like nothing. It wasn't like I scooped radioactive looking shit in my mouth, Jacks!"

"For someone who said they were going to try to be nicer, you sure have a weird way of showing it," Bex pinches my cheeks, and I glower up at her.

Niki snorts from where she's watching us, her delicate blue slippers dainty and feminine. "And then the dinosaur imprinted on you, because they're trained with lights as babies?"

"I haven't quite wrapped my head around that myself," I tell her.

"And you named him Steve," Bex crows, clearly delighted with me. "Of all the names, why Steve?"

"I was hungry, tired, and it was the first thing that popped in my head."

"I love the name Steve for a dinosaur," Carmen pipes up from where she's messing with the data she collected from me.

I pluck at the voluminous fabric of the pastel-colored dress that Bex called the shade of a sunrise at the beach. It's pink. Nothing wrong with pink. I like pink.

It's *aggressively* pink.

"This is what their women wore?" My lips twist to the side, imagining this shade of virulent pink on green skin.

"Nah, they mostly had blues and greens and yellows, but I sweet talked the fabric vendor into trying some new shades," Bex tells me.

"Of course, you did," I say.

"Pink is great on you, so shut up and let me get my hands on your hair." She rubs her palms together, a gleam in her eye. "You have no idea how long I've wanted to give you a makeover."

"There wasn't anything wrong with how I looked."

"I didn't say there was. But your hair is gorgeous, and I was afraid if I told you that, you'd make me run or worse, do plyometrics before giving me demerits."

I glare harder at her.

"Your face is going to get stuck like that, *Princess*." She runs her fingers through my nearly dry hair.

"Our chain of command has disintegrated," I tell Niki.

"Fuck the chain of command," she says cheerily.

"Fuck the Federation," Bex adds darkly.

"Fucking sounds like fun," Carmen sighs.

We all stare at her. "What's your story? What happened with your husband?"

She shrugs a shoulder. "I've barely seen him since we got to Edrobaz."

Niki clears her throat. "So, Gen. The warlord trials."

Carmen shoots her a grateful look.

"Yeah. What's that all about?" I stretch, grateful for soft, clean clothes, clean skin, and a roof overhead. Bex makes a disgruntled noise, tugging my hair around.

It's nice though. Sitting here, not worried about getting chomped by a mega snake, or a tentacle monster, with my friends. It's really fucking nice.

"I wanted to have status here, and not just because of Draz."

"Good for you," I say, popping one of the little snacks they brought out while I showered into my mouth.

She clears her throat again.

"Something getting stuck in there?" I narrow my eyes at her.

Carmen laughs.

"I just thought… they're in two weeks. Fourteen Suevan days. You are the princess now, and still our second in command. But I thought you might want to do the trials. In case you want to lead here, too."

"Oh." I pause, blinking at her. "That's a good idea."

"Abby and Juls are doing it with me, too."

"Good for them." I'm not too surprised to hear the newer recruits are interested in leveling up here. They're both smart and ambitious, and Niki and I talked at length about their potential before we left for Sueva.

And now that potential will stay on Sueva.

"Niki… you didn't know, right?"

"I wondered if you'd ask that." Her face is serious, none of the humor or good-natured warmth she usually radiates present. I glare at my glowing hands. I don't think I'll use the word radiate ever *again*.

"No, I didn't know. And I was so fucking mad. And worried about all of you. Draz and I were stuck in the jungle until last week, too. I didn't know where any of you were, and I felt so mad at myself for insisting everyone take part in that ceremony…" Her throat bobs, but she blinks rapidly, keeping the tears at bay. "If you're angry with me for giving the order, I understand."

"Don't be an idiot, Niki." My voice is soft, and my chest squeezes. "The Federation fucked us all over, but you especially." I shake my head. She was so proud and happy to have been picked to head up this mission, only for them to throw her away at the Suevans like so much garbage. "You should have been next up for a huge career bump, and instead they sold you off."

"And you, too."

"Yeah, but I've always been an asshole and a thorn in their side. I bet I was first on their list of women to sell off."

Niki snorts, but we both know it's true.

"How are the rest of the crew handling it?"

"Everybody's still adjusting," Bex says, combing her fingers through my hair. "It would be easier if our *husbands* weren't acting so fucking weird about it."

"What do you mean?"

"When they found out we'd been tricked, they refused to get near us. Besides, most of us still can't communicate."

"I want you to do the Warlord Trials with me, Gen," Niki interrupts, her attention focused on me. "I think it will be good for the crew to see us both in action again. Good for morale, and it might help everyone settle into their new lives here more easily. Going back isn't an option."

"She needs to take it easy," Carmen says.

"She's fine," Niki replies, arching an eyebrow at me. "Aren't you?"

"Nothing a good night or two of sleep can't fix." And some rigorous talk therapy, but I know that's not what she's asking about. "When are they, again?"

"Two weeks. Two weeks to train and get ready. We work as a team."

"Warrior princess Genevieve Durand," Bex interrupts, tugging at my hair.

"What do I have to do?" I say, because I can't say I'm not all in on this idea.

Niki's lips curve into an evil smile, and I grin back at her.

We're gonna kick some Suevan Warlord ass.

GEN

AFTER DROPPING by the main crew's myza and taking stock of how everyone's doing, Niki walks me through the streets of Edrobaz, pointing out the market and stopping to buy me a delicious, fizzy drink.

"I had a team sent to prep a myza for you and the prince to stay in," she says. "Just in case you weren't Stockholmed into liking him."

I roll my eyes at her. "Thanks, Jacks." I sip the drink, savoring the refreshing taste. "This is good."

"It's not all bad here," she says quietly, rubbing her arm. "I know that all of this is… horrible, frankly, but I want to help the women carve out a life here, with or without their husbands. It's the least I can do."

"Niki, stop." I take her by the arm, locking eyes with her. "None of this is your fucking fault. Those assholes at the Federation are the ones who take the blame."

"That doesn't mean I'm going to just forget about the crew and gallivant around Sueva with my hot husband while they suffer."

"Obviously not, but that doesn't mean you have to beat yourself up over a situation you had no part in."

"I am the *captain*. They are under *my* command. And their lives were *ruined* under my command."

"Because of our superior officers," I say softly, shaking her arm. "Don't do this to yourself."

She inhales, and it's a shaky breath. "Okay. I know you're right…"

"But it's hard. I hear you." We lapse into silence, the sound of muttered Suevan conversations babbling around us like water in a stream. As we walk, my glow draws a lot of irritating attention from the few Suevans shopping.

"Are you okay?" I finally ask her, as we round a corner to a quieter street. Lightning bugs the size of hummingbirds flit overhead, bobbing illumination that casts a soft light.

She heaves a sigh, then smiles. "I am more okay now that you're here. I was literally sick with worry over you. But I love Draz." She shakes her head, her expression rueful. "I never would have imagined this life for me, but I do love him. We'll figure the rest out as it comes." Her hand goes to her stomach.

"Here it is," she says, and my gaze flits to the myza in front of me. "And look, here they come."

Sure enough, two hulking Suevans stride toward us. Draz, with his huge sword and devilish scar, and my Kanuz, smirking and swaggering beside him. They're deep in conversation, but when Kanuz glances up and sees me, he does a double take, standing still as his gaze rakes over me.

Warmth heats my cheeks and chest, and Niki lets out a low laugh.

"I'll go ahead and leave you two, for now. There's a comm tablet in there with my info programmed in it already. I'll call you in the morning and we can train for the Trials together." She gives me an exaggerated wink, and I shove her shoulder as she laughs. "Don't get too frisky, Durand. We have *work* to do!"

With that, Draz scoops her up in a hug, and Kanuz finally gets a grip of himself, walking towards me as the oversized fireflies dip and swirl overhead.

"My flower," he says quietly, tucking a strand of stray hair behind my ear. I lean into the touch, smiling up at him.

He pushes the arched door open, and I sigh with relief at having him near again.

"The Roth is going to help," he says, closing the door softly behind us as though he hasn't just dropped the nuclear bomb of information.

"He what?!" I explode, my heart rate spiking as I stare, open-mouthed, at Kanuz. "You know as well as I do they can't be trusted."

"He has two brothers," Kanuz continues, running his hands through his hair. "They are entering Suevan territory now, in a small freighter. He bargained to help us save their lives."

"It's a trick," I exclaim, angry. I tug at the cropped, silky pink top they dressed me in, feeling stupid for being made up and draped in this silly dress. No wonder I stopped caring what I looked like. I don't feel like I can be taken seriously in all this, even though it made me feel pretty and put together for the first time in years.

"I understand your apprehension, Gen." He shakes his head slowly.

"You promised you'd rip out his spine for me!" I poke at his bare chest, and he catches my hand in his, some humor returning to his face.

"And you politely declined, if I recall correctly."

"That doesn't mean I think we should make an alliance with the Roth!"

"We are not making an alliance with the Roth. We are allowing one Roth's brothers to leave our space with their lives in exchange for strategic information against the Roth Overlord's operations." His lips purse, and I stand still, letting the information compute, letting it get through the cracks in my initial anger.

"I didn't think a Roth would even care about their family."

"I was likewise surprised. Perhaps, next time, you will accompany me on business and I will be spared your anger because we can decide together."

"Deal." I heave a sigh, finally taking in the interior of our temporary home. "This is nice," I say, changing the subject. I don't want to think about the Roth. Not right now, at least. Right now, I want to hang out with Kanuz. I want to sleep. I want to sleep with Kanuz as part of our hanging out.

"It is nothing compared to my palace at Perzivor, but it will do. Were your companions safe and sound?"

"They are... Kanuz, what do you know about the Warlord Trials?"

"They are the ultimate test of strength, courage, and intellect for our people. Those who make it to the end become the leaders of our cities."

"Niki is taking part in it. In two weeks... and I'm joining her." I narrow my eyes, waiting for him to say he doesn't want me to do it, that I'm a princess now or some other nonsense.

But Kanuz only grins wider, then clasps me to him. "I would be honored for my mate to be a warlord of Sueva. A princess and a warlord. Yes. I like that very much."

"You're not upset?"

"Why would I be upset?"

"Because... I didn't talk about it with you first?" I'm grasping at straws.

"You do not need to discuss every decision with me. I am honored to hear out any problems you have, but your life is yours, as much as you are my mate, you are still your own person, are you not?" He scratches his chin. "I am more and more concerned about what your marriages look like on Earth."

"I just thought you would be mad."

"Did you want to have a fight?" He raises one eyebrow, perplexed.

"No," I say, not sure what to do with my hands. "Of course, I didn't."

Suddenly, he slams me against the walls of the myza, caging me in with his broad arms on either side of me. "If it is a fight you want, my golden flower, I am happy to oblige your every whim. I did not know your passions had this edge, but I am more than willing to test how sharp you are."

My heart speeds up, and I'm suddenly wet with desire. His mouth ravishes mine, and when I reach up to cup his face, his hands circle my wrist. Before I can react, he's pressed them over my head, pinning them to the wall with one hand.

His other hand makes small circles on the exposed skin of my abdomen, his talons tickling at the seam of the blouse. "I like this outfit very much."

"It's different," I say, my eyes closing as he kisses the sensitive flesh of my neck. A shiver runs down my spine, and I let out a soft moan.

"You like it when I'm firm with you. When I'm in charge. I can tell. I can smell it on you. I can smell the greediness from that wet cunt of yours." His nose presses against the juncture of my neck and shoulder, and he inhales deeply, challenge in the statement.

My eyes fly open, and I'm more than game to rise to his challenge. "You want it like that, huh? You want to be in charge?"

"Are you going to let me, little flower?" His fangs graze my skin.

"Yes," I say, and then jerk my hands from his loosening grip. Or, at least, I try to.

"Ah, ah, ah," he murmurs. His lips curl into a smile against my neck, and then the pressure from his fangs increases. "You said you would let me."

His hand slips under the fabric of my blouse, and he growls in approval as his fingers caress the pointed tip of my breast.

I let myself sag against him, more excited than I'd ever imagine I'd be by this little roleplay. His fingers loosen slightly on my wrists, and I grind against him, searching for more. Needing him.

His grip loosens even more, and then I yank my hands away,

slipping under his arm and laughing wildly as my feet pad against the wood floor. I'm not fast enough though, not by far, and before I hit the doorway to the bedroom Kanuz is on me, his hands on my waist as he throws me over one shoulder.

I squeal, caught between laughter and arousal, and enjoying myself way too much. It's like a wildfire, this thing between me and Kanuz. I keep expecting it to burn out, to be all smoke, but it burns hard and fast and catches everything in its wake.

With one arm around my waist, he strides through the door, then slaps my ass, hard enough to make me cry out in surprise.

"Is that what you want, Gen? You want that?" His voice is husky and raw, and my amusement at our little foreplay turns molten and dangerous.

Before I can answer, he tugs the fabric from my hips, exposing my bare ass, the pink garment falling to the floor. He rubs the palm of his hand against it, and I moan softly. His hand leaves my skin, and for a moment, I tense, thinking he's going to spank me again.

But he doesn't. Instead, his talon-less finger slips inside me, and I go still against him, savoring the sensation.

"So fucking ready for me." He pulls his finger out, then tosses me on the bed, which I sink into, staring up at him as he licks my wetness from his hand.

He watches me with an avid gaze. We stay like that, waiting to see what the other will do. His chest rises and falls quickly, and I drink in the sight of him, his thickly muscled chest, the masculine set of his jaw, the full lips.

And then slowly, I spread my naked legs wide, daring him to touch me again. He's on me in seconds, his mouth pressed against my pussy, his blunt fingers sliding inside me as he teases all around my clit.

I grind against his face, already near senseless with pleasure, and my orgasm comes so quickly it takes me by complete surprise.

Kanuz stands and rips his pants off. "I fucking love that. I love you, Gen. I love the noises you make when I make you come. I love how fierce you are, how soft for me you become. I will never have enough of you."

"Kanuz," I say, holding my arms out to him. He pulls me to the edge of the bed, thrusting inside me quickly, filling me up so hard and fast that I have no time to adjust to his size, no time to get ready for the overwhelming pressure and vibrations of his xof as it continues to stimulate my clit.

His hands bracket my hips, and he slams into me, a feral look on his face, his eyes locked on mine. He bends down, sucking my nipple into his mouth, and I arch into him.

"Yes," I moan, "more."

"More," he growls, his teeth grazing the sensitive skin there, his hand slipping down the curve of my ass. I tense, but he makes a soothing noise, and then his fingers pressing against the tight pucker there, and as his xof vibrates, his mouth working my nipple, his cock deep inside me... It's too much.

It's enough.

I shatter, coming so hard that the world seems to fracture around me.

"That's right, my flower, come for me," he urges, releasing my breast and claiming my mouth with his, devouring my moans and incoherent sounds. "Come again. I know you can."

I don't think I can, but he slows his thrusts, laying me back on the bed and trailing small kisses over my face and neck, before flipping so I'm on top of him.

"I like this," he growls, holding me upright as I writhe, blissed out yet building towards more. He fondles my breasts, his xof vibrating so hard that it's all I can do not to fall into a limp orgasmed out puddle on top of him.

Instead, I lean forward and ride him, rising to his challenge.

"Now it's your turn," I whisper, closing my eyes as I lose myself to the rhythm of our bodies.

"Gen," he moans, and I finally slump over, worn out, as he continues to thrust, his cock jerking as he comes deep inside me.

We stay like that for a long while, until our breath evens out, until I can form coherent thoughts again.

"I love you." I kiss him slowly, and he returns it sweetly, cradling my head in his hands.

"I love you, too. Now you must get some sleep," he says, tugging me off him and placing me on the bed. He gets up gracefully, walking away.

"Where are you going?" I ask, sitting up abruptly.

"To get a cloth to clean you off with," he says, a confused look on his face. "Where else would I be going?"

"Oh. I don't know." I bite my lip, Niki and Bex's words of warning crashing through my head.

"You are lying," he says, irritation plain in his tone.

"Fine." I lie back, and he returns a moment later, wiping off the evidence of our sexcapades with a cool, wet cloth and gentle hands.

"Are you going to tell me what you were thinking when you made this face?" He scrunches up his face, puckering his lips, looking for all the world like he's just bitten into a lemon.

I burst out laughing. "I did not look like that."

"Well, you were also glowing," he says seriously, "but I cannot make my skin do that."

I whack him with one of the little pillows littered on the bed.

He waits, one eyebrow raised.

"Fine," I repeat, blowing out a breath. "The girls were telling me you have some kind of a reputation. They were worried about me."

"And do you care that your husband has a past?" His features are arranged in careful neutrality. "I already told you as much."

"Do you care that your wife has one?" I retort.

He takes my hand in his, pressing a kiss across my knuckles. "I only care that our future is together, my flower."

I crawl onto him, hugging him to me as he runs his fingers across my bare skin.

"I am proud of you for joining the Trials," he said. "No matter what happens."

"No matter what happens?" I ask, jerking my head up to look at him. "What, you think I survived the temple but can't survive a little Warlord Trial?" My chin juts out aggressively, the effect somewhat ruined by the fact he's jiggling my ass with his hands.

"Oh, I know for a fact you can and will. I just like it when you get mad, Indiana Jones."

I blink at him, then burst out laughing again, nestling under his chin. When I fall asleep in his arms, I'm smiling.

CHAPTER
TWENTY-SIX

KANUZ

MY GAZE SWINGS around the training yard, assessing the four females' stances. Draz assists Ni-kee, correcting the way she holds her sword. They are not used to using anything but knives and guns, but in the Trials, they'll need to be proficient with a sword, too.

Alvez and Dergoz are helping the other two females, who make up for what they lack in the finesse and skill of Ni-kee and Gen with pure youthful energy and what looks to be unfettered rage.

I'm not sure who the female they call Abby's wed to, but I plan to send a prayer up to the mother goddess on his behalf anyway.

Gen's skin sparkles with sweat and her ever-present glow, her brow furrowed in concentration.

"Adjust your weight," I tell her, and she complies, sinking more evenly into her stance. "Good, my flower."

She swipes her sword at me, and I barely block it in time.

We've only been at this for a week now, the trials looming in just seven days time, but already she's shown much improvement.

"Son of bitch," Abby cries out, throwing her sword down.

"Control your temper," Ni-kee yells at her. "You represent all of Earth here, am I understood?"

Abby nods her head, then blows out a huge breath, picking up her sword once more.

"Is it time for a snack break?" Bex's happy little voice echoes through the arena.

Dergoz, her husband, immediately swings his attention to where she stands at the edge of the training field, a platter full of treats in her hand. She's dressed in bright colors, looking pretty as a spring day, but Dergoz grunts in irritation, then storms out the other side, ignoring her completely. A Brute indeed.

Bex's face falls.

"Why is he such an asshole? It's not like anyone tricked *him* into marrying her." Gen says, sliding her energy sword into the scabbard at her back with a refined flick of the wrist she picked up so quickly it made my cock stand up straight.

"He will not talk about her." I shrug. "I do not know."

"Well, if anyone wants a snack," Bex says, her voice faltering. Gen nudges me with her elbow.

"Of course, we want snacks, Bex," she calls out, pulling me beside her.

Abby continues to practice her stances, but the rest of us file over to where the platter of treats rests on a small bench where Bex stands, wringing her hands together.

"This was really nice of you," Gen tells her.

"Do you think—" She bites her lip, then smiles brightly at all of us. "Never mind. Enjoy it, you guys definitely deserve it. I'll just go back and help Michelle with her research."

She leaves, walking so swiftly away she's nearly running from the training ring.

Draz shoots me an irritated look.

"What the fuck is Dergoz's problem?" Gen says, clearly not caring who she offends. "Bex is so fun, and sweet, and pretty, and he's just going to ignore her forever? Does he want to divorce her?

He's making it worse." She grumbles something under her breath, then shoves whatever it is Bex brought into her mouth.

"Oumughud," she says through the mouthful, crumbs flying from her lips. She swallows, then wipes the back of her hand on her mouth. "They taste like chocolate chip cookies."

Niki grabs one, then takes a huge bite of it. "Heaven," she finally pronounces. "Abby, put your sword up and get over here."

Abby frowns at Ni-kee but does as she asks.

"What are chocolate chip cookies?" I ask Draz, rubbing the back of my neck.

"Probably can-dee," he says wisely. "Ni-kee loves can-dee."

"My mate likes to eat can-dee shaped like small children," I tell him.

Draz stares at me, horror struck. "Is this true?"

Ni-kee coughs, and Gen slaps her on the back, and then all the females are laughing.

"Sour Patch Kids?" Ni-kee finally croaks. "Oh my god."

"I didn't stop and think about how an alien species would react to that particular candy, okay?"

"Small children," the black-haired one called Juls wheezes. "I can't. I can't."

"Is that not what you call kids? Are they not small children?" Affronted, I hold my hands out, waiting for one of them to correct me. They all laugh harder, clutching at each other.

Draz shoots me a look of sympathy.

"Okay, but we need to do something about Bex and Dragoz," Gen finally says when the laughter slows down.

"We cannot," Draz says. "They will need to figure it out on their own."

"And how's that working out for them?" Gen asks, her tone dripping with acid. I snort.

"She's right," Ni-Kee says. "How can they work it out when he refuses to even see her?"

"We could mediate, considering her translator isn't working," Gen says slowly.

Alvez laughs at this, shaking his head. "Dergoz would rather Crigomar shit; I can tell you that much. There's a reason we call him the Brute."

"And the one they call the Beast?" Abby takes another bite of the cookie, and I realize that must be who her husband is. The Warlord known as the Beast is… unstable at best.

I sniff one of the treats Bex brought, but it smells much too sweet for my liking. I put it back, drawing Gen into my chest instead.

She is the perfect amount of sweetness for me. Not too much. Just right.

"The Beast will be here for the trial. All the Warlords will," Draz says slowly. Abby lowers the cookie, putting it back on the plate half-eaten. Without a word, she strides back into the ring, picking up the exercises right where she left off.

"That bad, huh?" Gen says.

Juls, or Juliana, I cannot remember which name she prefers, raises her eyebrows but says nothing.

Gen narrows her eyes at her, and Ni-Kee clears her throat.

"We're not all lucky like you," she finally spits out, realizing she's caught everyone's attention.

In the ring, Abby grunts, sweat slicking her face.

"Most of us have hardly seen our *husbands*," she adds, the word full of derision. "Bex tries, but you saw it. Only Michelle seems to be able to communicate with hers, and that's still awkward as fuck." Her eyes widen. "No offense."

"We're past that," Ni-Kee says, and Gen snorts a laugh. "We'll figure it out. We will."

"Yeah, well, I have it figured out. I'm going to be a Warlord, then no one can sell me off ever again." Juls wipes her hands off on her pants, then storms away, joining Abby in the ring.

"Well, this is pretty fucked," Gen remarks, squeezing my hands.

"It'll work out," Ni-Kee tells her, but her face is pinched with worry.

"It will, my heart," Draz adds, smiling gently at her. "They will come around. Kanuz and I will have a talk with the Warlords when they've returned here for your trials. Come now, let us return to training. I have a reputation to uphold, after all."

"Oh, do you, now?" Ni-Kee says, and there's a challenge in her eyes.

"Are you ready, my flower?" I ask Gen. "If you like, we can go back to our temporary myza. I have a few training activities in mind that might be more fun."

"Oh yeah? Lemme guess," she purses her lips, "advanced sword work?"

I frown at her. "No. I meant sex. I was talking about sex."

She throws her head back, laughing. "I know. That was the joke. You know what? Nevermind. Yours was funnier." She turns, walking back to the training ring. "Come on, we have work to do. We'll practice the horizontal mambo later."

"I do not know this mambo."

"We can do it vertically, too, I guess." She winks at me, her hair and skin glistening in the sun, and we take our positions across from each other.

There is nowhere I'd rather be than across from my small beauty, with the promise of a fight followed by pleasure.

GEN

At the Trials: One week later

"This fucking sucks," Abby yells, barely dodging one of the boulders raining down in the arena. She slides through a pit of muck on the floor, a swinging energy axe nicking the top of her ponytail.

"Goddamnit, I just grew my hair out."

Juls extends her hand, and Abby pulls herself up to stand next to Niki and me, huddled against a stone pillar. Several miniscule drones buzz around us, televising our every move to where the gathered crowd of Suevans and our human crew watch.

They're annoying, but after nearly twenty-four hours in the arena, I hardly notice them.

It's fucking intense.

Less so than the temple Kanuz and I were stuck in, but nobody was watching us then. If we fucked up and died horribly, there wouldn't be anyone to jeer at us. Except the zeloth, I guess, but the tentacle monster didn't look up to telling many tall tales.

"Focus, Gen. How many do you see?"

I exhale, peeking out from the stone column, managing to scrape it across my cheek. We're in the last stage of the Trials, and so far, all four of us have done all right for ourselves. I was worried about Abby making it through the boulder field, but she did it.

"Five." An energy projectile whizzes by my face, and I duck just in time. It explodes off a column behind us, sending up smoke and paint.

According to Kanuz and Draz, nothing in here is truly deadly, but I'm not sure I believe him. Deadly to a Suevan and deadly to a human are not exactly measured the same, in my experience.

"Five?" Juls repeats, blanching. "But there are only four of us."

"Gen has the weapon she picked up off the Suevan we dispatched earlier," Niki says calmly, nodding at me. "Gen takes point. Gen, pick off as many as you can. Juls, you go second. Run for the exit, don't get bogged down in a fight."

Juls, to her credit, doesn't argue. She's hanging in there, but she twisted her ankle in one of the climbing courses earlier, and her face is still slightly green.

"Abby, you go third. Try to get Juls out safely if she falls. No one gets left behind. I'll go last, and I'll try to sweep anyone out with me who falters. Got it?"

We all nod, our unquestioning faith in Niki's leadership on full display.

Another projectile crashes at our feet, and Abby coughs, the smoke and sparks exploding outward. This one came from behind us.

"Fuck," Abby says, scrambling forward. "On our six!"

"Gen, *MOVE!*" Niki yells.

I do as she says, shouldering my energy rifle. It only has a few pulses left, according to the charger on it. I focus down the sight, ready to take out anyone who moves.

But as soon as I enter the next room, the rifle fucking dies. I click the trigger, annoyance and adrenaline ramping up.

A Suevan, at least three feet taller than me, bounds into my path, his tail slashing through the air behind him.

"Fuck me," I say, throwing the energy rifle in his face as he lunges for me. Sharp talons slice at the thick leather-like vest protecting my torso, but I evade most of his grip.

"Gun's out!" I yell. "Gun is out!"

"Fuck," Juls shouts, running by me as best as her swollen ankle will allow. A second Suevan darts out of the shadows, tackling her to the ground.

"Goddammit," I yelp.

Then I see it: a sword, dull and unprimed, hanging from one of the walls.

I dive into a roll, earning a slap to the face with the massive Suevan's tail, then use my momentum to jump up, prying the sword from where it hangs on the wall.

"Fuck RIGHT OFF," Niki yells, and then there's a soft grunt as her fist connects with another Suevan's crotch. Her Suevan goes down hard, and she holds up her fist, where there's a rock clenched in it.

Good for her.

I prime the energy sword with a few clicks, and it whirs to life, the blade coated in a green haze, meaning it will stun and hurt, but won't kill.

It's going to have to be enough.

Juls is screaming on the floor, where a Suevan drags her by her bad foot out of the room. She's still giving him hell, her face contorted in fury, as she hammers kick after kick to his shin with her good leg.

"Fucking let her go!" I scream, launching myself at him. His gaze darts to me, surprise rocketing across his features as he realizes I am absolutely batshit crazy. "Too late, asshole!"

The sword smashes against his face, and his eyes roll back in his head as he goes down.

"Ah, fuck, thank you," Juls breathes.

"Stay down," I scream at her, way too amped up on adrenaline now to modulate anything about me at all.

Juls nods, her eyes wide, and I turn back to the chaos in the room. Niki's surrounded by three Suevans, who circle her, trying to find an opening.

But Abby?

Abby is white as a sheet, staring at the oversized Suevan who nearly snatched me when my gun died.

"They did not tell me you were competing," he's saying in a low snarl, but Abby's lip curls in rage, and I know that bitch is out for blood.

"Wife, I did not know you would be here," he continues, and Abby's gaze darts to me, her eyes narrowing as she sees the sword. Then she's off and running, to where a second sword hangs on the wall.

Her humongous husband watches her run, his pout turning wry as he realizes she's about to kick his ass or go out trying.

When he cracks his knuckles, I turn my attention back to Niki. Three on one is not great odds, but they're dancing around her still. Playing with her.

I grind my molars.

"Niki, let's do the merengue," I yell at her.

"I hate the merengue," she grits out, lashing a hand at a Suevan who steps too close.

Then I see it. A pile of the projectiles they were lobbing at us, to try and force us into this room.

"Forget the merengue," I scream at her. "Time for the limbo!"

Her gaze darts to me, and one of the Suevan's lashes out, catching her shoulder. She goes down hard, and my hand closes over one of the fake energy grenades.

"Stay down," I screech, and then I let it fly. It hits the closest Suevan, and he frowns at me as it explodes, then sits down heavily. *Out.* "Varsity softball, bitch!" I tell him, then pitch another into the Suevan leering over Niki.

It smacks him on the head, and he doesn't feign the pain on his face.

Now there's just one, flexing his shoulders as he measures the distance between us.

Two, if I count Abby's husband.

She's screaming obscenities at him, slashing wildly as he half-heartedly parries her attempts.

"Cool your tits, Abby, focus." I'm running towards Niki as I shout it at her, the sword in one hand and the energy grenade in the other. The Suevan backs away from her prone form as I close in, laughing maniacally.

At the last second, Niki's legs scissor out, catching the Suevan off guard and sending him falling back into one of the stone walls. I pitch the last grenade in his face for good measure, and it explodes in sparks and smoke when it hits his forehead.

"You're OUT," I say, and Niki snorts, standing uneasily.

"One left," Niki pants, tilting her chin at where Abby's winded and tired.

She cries out in pain as her Suevan husband—the Beast—lashes out a lazy stroke at her.

I squint. It didn't look like he made contact, and when I glance at Niki, her face reflects my confusion.

But Abby is screaming and carrying on as though she's mortally wounded.

"I wonder if she played soccer," Niki speculates.

"Should I…"

"Nah, let it happen."

Abby is sobbing softly, pressing her arm to her abdomen and glancing at it like she expects blood to pour out at any moment.

"Oscar worthy," I mutter, impressed.

The Suevan steps closer, a stricken expression on his face. Abby pants, her forehead screwed up and eyes shut, and as he tries to take a closer look, her hand darts out, lightning fast.

She grabs his balls and *twists*.

"Oh, shit," Niki says.

"Yeah," I agree.

"Get him!" Juls yells, dragging herself towards the exit door.

As for the Suevan, he's on his knees before her, so tall his head's still at her chest height.

She goes to kick him in the nuts again, but he catches her leg, twisting her to the floor.

"That's enough of that," I mutter, surging forward to slice at him with my energy sword. "You're done. You're done."

He frowns down at where Abby pants, murder written all over her face.

"Y'all need therapy," I tell her, offering her my hand. "You can't lose your cool like that," I add, pushing her to the door.

Niki's managed to haul Jul's over her shoulder, fireman style, and then we're limping out the exit, the Suevan Trials completed. We're bruised, battered, and bitchier than ever, but we finished.

We fucking did it.

TWENTY-EIGHT

KANUZ

NIKI EMERGES FIRST from the arena door, a tired but pleased looking Juls draped over her shoulder. We all witnessed her fall, cringing as the vid bots displayed the injury, scanning her immediately. Hairline fracture. Human bodies are so much more breakable than ours, and it made me want to run after Gen and pluck her from the course.

But Juls is in good spirits, and she's won the hearts of Sueva for powering through despite her obvious pain. The human medics, Carmen and Tati, are standing by with a Suevan med specialist to help patch her up.

Then Abby races through, her face grim and eyes flashing with anger. That one... that one is a female to watch. The way she dispatched the Beast was sneaky and mean, and I have a feeling that Draz is already making plans for how to best utilize our youngest female Warlord.

Gen's glowing face appears next, smudged with dirt and blood, her vest torn where talons ripped through it. She drops the practice energy sword, and squeals as she races into my arms.

My heart clenches as she jumps up, wrapping her legs around me, peppering kisses across my mouth. She tastes like sweat and blood and hard work, and I savor every press of her lips against mine.

"I am so fucking proud of you," I tell her, staring into her dazzling blue eyes.

"I did it!" she crows, and I support her weight as she pumps her fist into the air. "Oof, I'm sore already."

"You took some serious hits." I grin at her. "Like a Warlord."

"Like a badass bitch!" Niki yells, and all the women cheer.

The Beast of Sueva comes through the door as they're whooping, and Gen stiffens in my arms.

He looks proud though, swaggering out like he's won the prize and not just been trounced by four small human females.

Abby tenses in the corner, where the med techs work on scanning her and shooting her full of supplements.

The Beast is there in an instant, scooping her up. "That was a nasty trick, wife," he says, his voice low and rough.

Her eyes are huge in her dirty face, and they widen further when he kisses her.

Only to be rewarded with a swift kick to his abdomen.

He laughs darkly, and Abby's face is screwed up with rage.

"Put her down," Niki says, her voice dangerous. "Now." Draz steps closer to the pair, his tail lashing back and forth.

The Beast does as she bids, setting her down. Abby watches him with a guarded gaze, and he lashes out a talon, causing her to flinch, but all he does is run it across her cheek before turning with a laugh.

She glares at his back as he leaves the room.

"Okay, then," Gen says as the door snicks shut. "Who's ready to party?"

Bex bursts through the door at the same instant, jumping up and down, the rest of their crew pouring in, surrounding the newest Warlords and first humans to make it through our trials, cheering and clapping them on the back.

Gen squeezes my hand once, then allows the crowd of women to sweep her away from me.

I love seeing her happy. I love that something here on Sueva has made her so pleased.

She's one of us now. A Warlord. A princess.

She's mine.

CHAPTER
TWENTY-NINE

GEN

THE PARTY'S RAUCOUS, everyone drinking more of the potent Suevan alcohol than is likely healthy for humans. Our entire crew is on the dance floor, even Juls, who's being half-carried around by Bex and Michelle like the conquering hero she is.

Niki and Draz are locked in each other's embrace, swaying together slowly despite the upbeat tempo of the Suevan music.

Bex keeps casting longing looks at Dergoz, who seems to ignore her completely, except... every once in a while, I see him staring at her, too. Maybe there's hope for those two, after all.

Michelle and Alvez also manage to ignore each other almost completely. Michelle, because she seems genuinely oblivious to the way he keeps watching her. Alvez, apparently, because he doesn't know what the hell to do with the brainy beauty. Hell, she intimidates me, and I've been her superior officer for years.

It's Abby, though, who I keep glancing toward. The Beast, her husband, showed up, to everyone's surprise, but the tension quickly faded as he made a beeline for Abby, who was already nice and toasty on Suevan alcohol.

Now they're kissing, and truly, the woman has set a new bar for public displays of affection. I'm half-afraid they're going to start humping in the dark corner

"Can you make sure she doesn't go home with him?" I ask, biting my lip. "I don't want her to do anything she regrets, and I watched her drink at least three cups of the alien go-go juice."

"Go-go juice?" Kanuz repeats.

"Jungle punch. Trash can whack. Girl's going to have a hangover from hell."

"I will have the others make sure she is safe. But you need not worry. The Beast looks fearsome, but he holds the same morals as the rest of us. He will not take advantage of her." Kanuz holds me gently, his hands on my hips as we both face the gleeful dancers.

I relax slightly, averting my eyes as Abby writhes against the huge alien.

"Do you not want to dance, my flower?" he asks softly, his lips brushing my earlobe. "You do not seem as celebratory as I imagined you would."

I avoided the alcohol tonight, my stomach weird and unsettled, and simply thinking about it makes me nauseated. I lean my head against his shoulder, glancing up at him and smiling.

"Honestly, Kanuz, I'm ready for bed." And I am. I am beat. I don't know if it's because of the stress of the last twenty-four odd hours in the Trials, or relief, or something else, but I am completely wiped.

"My Warlord is insatiable," he murmurs, nibbling on my ear, and I chuckle.

"No, your Warlord is pooped," I tell him.

"You are what?" His voice is aghast, and when I turn to look at him, his mouth is curled in disgust.

I can't help laughing harder. "Oh my God. No. It means tired. I'm tired. I am completely exhausted. Take me to bed, Prince, but like, I just wanna sleep."

"Say no more," he says, pulling my hand and leading me from the throng of Suevans and humans celebrating their new

Warlords. "I will give you a massage. I will loosen all your muscles, and you will fall asleep in my arms."

"Mmm," I say, looping my arm around his hips. "That sounds perfect."

The sounds of music and revelry begin to fade behind us as we walk through the illuminated streets of Edrobaz.

I pause, my mouth suddenly full of saliva. I gag, one hand flying to my mouth, the other gripping Kanuz's bicep.

"Oh, no," I mutter. But I can't stop it, and I lurch to the side, throwing up all over the street.

"What is wrong?" Kanuz is frantic, and I go to my knees, heaving again, as he freaks out.

"Carmen," I tell him. "Get Carmen."

He's gone in an instant, and I sit on my knees, wiping my mouth, feeling, of all the things, idiotic. Like I'm stupid for throwing up.

Because even though I'm still weak and nauseated, I mostly feel better.

I don't want to ruin anyone's night.

Carmen appears, trailed by Michelle and clutching her little med kit the Suevans use.

"Shit," she says, taking one look at me, my blue dress dirty where it trails in the street next to where I hunch over a pool of sick. "Did you hit your head? In the Trials?"

"No," I shake it, then regret the motion instantly. "Not that I remember."

"Are you having memory loss problems? What day is it?"

I rattle off the Suevan date, just as another wave of nausea hits me. I dry-heave, but nothing comes up, and Kanuz puts something cool on the back of my neck, his tail slamming back and forth on the street.

"Did you eat anything weird? Anything unusual?"

I shake my head, stars swimming before my eyes, and Kanuz leans me against his big body, holding me upright.

"Ah, okay." Carmen frowns, and Michelle passes her the

portable med scanner. "We didn't see any pathogens in you when we scanned you after the Trials, but maybe it took time to develop."

"Are you super tired?" Michelle asks suddenly, her eyes owlish in her face.

"Yes," I say, Kanuz nodding his head in agreement.

"Have you been wanting to eat anything strange?" Michelle continues.

Carmen stares at her, then at me. "When was your last period?"

"Her what?" Kanuz asks.

My jaw drops open. "No."

"Well, we'll find out in a minute," Carmen says, and a needle appears in her hand. She grabs my wrist, pricking my index finger without so much as a please or thank you.

I think she must be as shocked as I am.

"I have an IUD," I tell her.

"They're not perfect tech," she says.

"What are you talking about? What is wrong with her?" Kanuz's voice is frantic, and I can't even answer him. My mind is spinning.

Michelle simply glances between us, astonishment clear on her face.

The machine beeps a moment later.

"Holy hell," Carmen says.

"That's not very professional," Michelle admonishes.

"It's positive," I say faintly, my hand flying to my abdomen.

"What is she positive for? Tell me, my flower, and I will do everything in my power to cure you. We will travel to all the galaxies. I would negotiate with the Roth Overlord himself."

"That won't be necessary," Carmen says, a beaming smile on her face. "She'll be cured in about nine and half months." Her mouth twists to the side. "Well, that is, if your gestation period is as long as human pregnancies. There are a lot of unknowns in an interspecies pregnancy like this."

"An interspecies pregnancy?" Kanuz repeats, his tone confused. "She is, you mean to tell me," he sputters, his hands taking mine. "My flower?"

"We're going to have a baby," I tell him, starting to tear up. Then I throw up again, and Carmen steps back.

"Damn. Okay. We're going to have to figure out something for your morning sickness," she says. "Vitamin B…" She trails off, tapping her screen. "Maybe an antihistamine. Might make you sleepy."

"I'm already sleepy," I say, then prove it with a jaw-cracking yawn.

I don't think it's sunk in yet.

A baby. I'm pregnant. With a *baby*.

"I want to take you to the med center and get a look at that IUD."

"Tomorrow," I tell her, drooping into Kanuz's arms.

"Right now," he says. "We're going right *now*."

"Right now it is," Carmen says nervously.

"You're scaring her," I admonish.

"You are scaring me," he says, and I notice for the first time that his greenish coloring is paler than usual.

"It's just a baby," I say. "A baby," I repeat, a soft smile stealing over my face.

"Our baby," he says. And with that, he picks me up again, and we're following Carmen to the med center.

At this rate he's never going to let me walk again.

EPILOGUE

GEN

I CAN'T STOP TOUCHING my stomach. According to the Suevan medical team and Carmen, the baby's growth rate is slightly accelerated compared to humans, explaining why I had such a quick onset of pregnancy symptoms.

The mirror shows a slight tiny bump, like I ate too many burritos, not like I'm carrying the first half-human half-Suevan child. Still, I touch it tenderly.

"Little burrito, what are you going to look like?"

"First, you tell me humans eat food shaped like children, and now you call our baby after food? Truly, my flower, it is disturbing."

I snort a laugh, and Kanuz's hand curls around the curve of my stomach. I stare at our reflection in the mirror for a moment. I'm still glowing, as I apparently will for the next decade or so, if not more, according to all the lab work I've had done, and Kanuz's green scales reflect some of the shine. His handsome face rests on the top of my head, his fingers stroking my stomach so gently it makes my heart ache.

"We should go visit our first baby," I tell him.

It's his turn to laugh, and he raises his eyebrows at my reflection. "That thing is far from a baby."

"I know, I know, but he misses me."

"I did stop by the butcher for him."

I clap my hands, and turn to face him. "Steve is going to be so thrilled you thought of him."

"Steve only has eyes for you, my warrior princess. And I cannot say I blame him one bit." He kisses my forehead.

By the time we get to Steve's temporary living situation in the jungle, I'm winded.

"Tell me again about the Roth?" I ask, then cup my hands around my mouth. "STEVE! WE BROUGHT YOU A SNACK!"

The dinosaur—Crigomar—trumpets a response, and the nearby trees shake as he pounds through the jungle towards us.

"His intel has been good so far," Kanuz admits grudgingly. "I would love it if you took a look at what he's told us, but I know you've been feeling ill."

It's true, and it's annoying. I've been barely able to hold any food down, despite all the concoctions Carmen's injected me with in the last week. She says it's a good thing, though, that it means my hormone levels are high and that everything is progressing well with the baby.

Steve finally pops into view, his red and black hide near invisible in the deep jungle.

"Hi, baby," I croon at him. "Look what Daddy brought you."

"I am not his father," Kanuz replies, his expression long-suffering.

"I know, but just go with it, Prince."

Kanuz tosses the hunk of meat to Steve, who chomps it out of the air like a good dog. Except, you know, he's an alien T-Rex who weighs close to eight tons. Bone fragments fly through the air, and Steve makes happy eating noises as he nudges closer to me, finally curling up and regarding me with big, black eyes as he chews.

I scratch the bridge of his nose, and a deep purring growl sounds.

"Are you excited?" I ask suddenly.

We've both been so caught up in the surprise of it, in trying to figure out what I can eat and our duties as Warlord and Prince, that we've hardly had downtime to really talk about what it means for us.

"To be a father? To our actual child, and not the Crigomar?" The questions are astounded, and he grabs my wrist, tugging me to him.

Steve whuffs his disapproval.

"My flower, I have never been more excited in my entire life. And afraid. And thrilled. And happy." He tilts his head, studying me. "And you? Are you excited?"

I take a deep breath, glad that we waited a week to have this conversation. At first, I was too shocked to feel anything. Then I was terrified.

But now?

Now I look at Kanuz and I see the male I love. I look at the Suevan jungle and the beautiful city of Edrobaz, and it's starting to feel like home. It feels more safe than Earth ever did, that's for sure.

Even with the Roth in the holding cells.

"I'm so happy, it makes me almost scared," I tell Kanuz quietly.

Steve spits out a bone, and Kanuz's lip curls in disgust and amusement.

"Do not be scared, Gen. I am not going anywhere. We will stay in Edrobaz, where you have your friends, until you are ready to move to my Perzovir. In fact..." his lips twitch to the side, and I narrow my eyes at him.

"What? Spill it."

"My father is planning a trip here. To meet you. He was quite impressed with the footage from the Trials. He was even more impressed to hear that we bested one of the ancient temples."

"Oh." I angle my head, considering him. "How do you feel about that?" I know that Kanuz's father, the king, is a bit of a sore spot for him.

"I feel proud," he says slowly, running a hand through my hair. "I cannot wait to show him my glowing bride, swelling with my child. The woman who is Warlord and Princess both, with a fearsome Crigomar for a pet. I think... I think our king will love you as much as I do."

I wrap my arms around him, pulling him tight to me.

"I'm glad we're not leaving Edrobaz yet. Thank you."

"I do not want to stress your human body," he says.

"That's not why I'm excited," I say, smirking and pulling away to pet Steve some more. He closes his eyes in appreciation, his black and red tail thwacking the trees.

"Then why?" Kanuz asks, his brow furrowed.

"Because I can't wait to see how Bex is going to pull off her plan to make Dergoz fall in love with her."

He groans, a pained sound, as he rubs a hand over his face. "How many times must I tell you both this is a terrible idea?"

I laugh, and it's an evil, villainous sound that makes Steve look around. Bex and I have been planning this for days, since I've been too sick to do much and she's appointed herself my personal valet, which is too much fun to say no to.

"No risk, no reward," I tell him, still grinning wickedly.

"Yes," he says, sidling closer and pulling me back into his arms. "I think we did prove that, didn't we?"

When he kisses me, all thoughts disappear from my mind.

Funnily enough, I'm totally okay with that.

Click here to read a bonus epilogue feature Gen and Kanuz meeting Kanuz's dad, the king!

If you enjoyed reading this book, please consider leaving a

review. Reviews help indie authors be seen by new readers, which means I get to keep writing!

To never miss a release, sign-up for my newsletter here.

Check out Bex's book, Wed To The Alien Brute.

ALSO BY JANUARY BELL

ACCIDENTAL ALIEN BRIDES

Wed To The Alien Warlord

Wed To The Alien Prince

Wed To The Alien Brute

Wed To The Alien Gladiator

Wed To The Alien Beast

Wed To The Alien Assassin

Wed To The Alien Hunter

Wed To The Alien Rogue

ALIEN DATING GAMES

Alien Tides

BOUND BY FIRE

Alien On Fire

FATED BY STARLIGHT

Following Fate: Prequel Novella

Claimed By The Lion: Book One

Stolen By The Scorpio: Book Two

Taurus Untamed: Book Three

ABOUT THE AUTHOR

January Bell writes steamy sci-fi romance with a guaranteed happily ever after. Combining pure escapism, a little adventure, and a whole lotta love makes for romance that's a world apart. January spends her days writing, herding kids and ducks, and spends the nights staring at the stars.

For the latest updates, follow me on Instagram and Tiktok.

www.ingramcontent.com/pod-product-compliance
Lightning Source LLC
Chambersburg PA
CBHW061348310726
48974CB00001B/255